GUINEVERE

I hope you enjoy starting Guinevere and Cedwyn!

On the

Eve of

Legend

Cheryl Carpinello

Outskirts Press, Inc.
Denver, Colorado

To Cameron Robert

May you grow up reading

Special Thanks to

Louise Guillaudeu

TABLE OF CONTENTS

PROLOGUE

Many centuries ago in the country of England, there lived a princess. Her name was Guinevere. She loved being a princess because she didn't have duties. She just had adventures with her best friend Cedwyn. They would roam the plains surrounding the castle looking for mythical creatures like unicorns or hoping to discover new lands. But their favorite adventure was hunting for rabbits in the forest.

Guinevere's father King Leodegrance ruled over a small part of southern England. After the death of her mother, he tried to give her an education to prepare her for the future. He even enlisted the help of his friend Merlyn, the wizard, to educate her in worldly matters because one day Guinevere would be a queen. Guinevere knew that, and it didn't bother her. A girl of twelve, she looked no further ahead than to what new adventure and fun each day would bring. She had no idea of the changes coming in her life.

CHAPTER 1
THE HUNT

Guinevere stared into the shadows along the edge of the forest. She could hear Cedwyn shifting from foot to foot beside her, unable to stand still. She sighed, the bow made of sturdy pine in her hand growing heavier like her heart. Her thirteenth Birth Day was in a few days, but she wasn't excited. Birth Days were supposed to be fun, but not this year. Not for her, not for a princess.

She frowned as Cedwyn adjusted the leather quiver of arrows on his back again. Sometimes, like today, her patience with the seven-year-old was short.

"Guin'ver?"

"Hush!"

"But ..."

"Hush!"

She stamped her boot on the ground, her displeasure clearly showing.

"Cedwyn," she snapped. "What is so important that you can't be quiet?"

"I'm hungry, and the bottoms of my trousers are wet. Can't we

1

go back to the castle?" His face showed his confusion at her tone.

Guinevere realized that she shouldn't have directed her anger at Cedwyn. It wasn't his fault. Glancing down at her own clothes, she saw the bottom of her green ankle-length tunic wet with the morning dew. Her stomach chose that moment to begin grumbling. It started as a low vibration but grew louder as if it hadn't been fed in days. Cedwyn heard it and started giggling. He tried to smother the sound by covering his mouth with his small hand, but he was too late.

Trying to keep from laughing also, Guinevere shook her head. "How are we ever going to shoot a rabbit with all this noise?" She reached down and tousled his blond hair to let him know that she was not serious and to apologize for her crossness. "Let's try for just ten minutes longer. Then if we find nothing, we'll go back. Is that all right?"

Cedwyn shook his head, not wanting to make any further noise.

She let her eyes move across the blue sky. The English summer sun had barely reached above the far hills when they had first arrived at the forest. Now, it was well on its way in its climb toward the dinner hour, and they hadn't even had a proper breakfast yet. Cedwyn's mum was sure to be upset that they had been gone so long.

"Come on," he whispered. "The only creatures we've seen moving have been badgers and Cornish hens. We could of had five bloody hens by now."

"I told you, it's good luck to bag a rabbit on the eve of your thirteenth Birth Day," Guinevere informed him.

Cedwyn studied her face, unsure if she was telling the truth or not. Then his blue eyes widened, and he grabbed her arm as she turned to continue hunting. "Wait a minute! You promised to help me bag a rabbit on the eve of my tenth Birth Day. You said that was lucky!"

She turned to him, her balled fists on her slim hips. "You need to listen closer when I talk to you. I explained the difference between boys and girls. Boys have to seek luck on the eve of their tenth and fifteenth Birth Days. Since girls are naturally luckier than boys, they only have to seek luck once, on the eve of their thirteenth Birth Day."

Cedwyn eyed her suspiciously, and then his eyes lit up.

"But I thought that the eve was the night before. Your Birth Day isn't until the day after tomorrow."

"That's true, but the eve of something can also be anytime close to the day."

"Are you sure?"

"Of course I am! Otherwise, what would happen if the day before I didn't get a rabbit? This way there are more chances to get one. Now, let's go. I'm sure I saw the grass moving up ahead, and I don't think it was the wind." She didn't mention to him that she needed lots of luck.

Cedwyn obediently followed her, mumbling to himself. "We're still running out of time."

They hadn't gone far when he thought of something else.

"Guin'?"

She turned suddenly, her long brown braid whipping about. "Shh! You will scare the rabbits away!"

"But you also promised to teach me how to hunt with a bow and arrow once you are thirteen."

"Yes, but if you don't stop your chatter, I won't. Do you understand?" Cedwyn nodded. "Then let's go."

He followed, a smile highlighting his chubby cheeks. He then smacked into Guinevere who had abruptly stopped.

"Wha..." A hand clamped down over his mouth followed by an angry "Shh!"

Cedwyn moved quietly up to her side, his seven-year old frame about half the size of Guinevere. She looked down at him, excitement making her brown eyes sparkle in the midmorning light. Her lips formed the word "Look." His blue eyes followed her outstretched arm.

There, just beneath the pine trees where the wild grasses grew-- movement. He stared at the spot. Then the tall green stalks bent again, betraying the presence of something beneath.

"How can you tell if it's really a rabbit?" he asked softly.

"See how the stalks move forward a bit and then part?" Cedwyn nodded. "Well, the forward movement of the stalks is the

3

rabbit testing out the goodness of the food. And then where the grasses part---that is---when the rabbit stops and starts feeding," Guinevere said, her pride in her knowledge showing. "Hand me an arrow." She held out her hand as Cedwyn pulled an arrow from the small leather quiver on his back.

Very carefully, her heart pounding, Guinevere nocked the arrow and steadily drew the bow string back. Taking a deep breath to steady her arms and calm her heart, she let the arrow loose. She watched the spin of the feathers as the arrow sped to its target like a hawk diving after its prey.

Suddenly a horrendous cry filled the air. Guinevere and Cedwyn jumped into each other's arms. Then they knelt down on the ground and covered their ears as the shrill cry continued to make their ears ring.

"Wh...what is that?" Cedwyn whispered.

Guinevere shook her head in reply.

Then they heard a different sound. Something was crashing through the grasses and scrub thickets. They inched their way up to peek above the grass. There, crashing and charging around the thickets, was the biggest wild boar they had ever seen.

Cedwyn looked at Guinevere. "Ain't that your arrow sticking in its side?"

She nodded, almost appearing disinterested, but really in shock that she had hit anything. For a few moments, they watched as the boar ran first in one direction and then another in what appeared to be a crazed pattern. But Guinevere recognized the pattern: the wounded boar was searching for its hunters.

"Come on," she said, grabbing his hand. "We have to get out of here now!"

"Why?"

But then he had his answer. The boar roared in anger. The ground trembled under their feet as the boar spotted them and barreled straight for them. It had found the culprits responsible for the arrow in its side.

"Run!" Guinevere said, no longer quiet.

Cedwyn needed no further urging. He took off with Guinevere close behind him. The thunderous crashing of the boar through the grasses and scrub brush vibrated through every part of their bodies.

Guinevere chanced a look behind her and realized that the boar was gaining on them. She glanced around. Off to the right was a smaller pine tree that Cedwyn could climb to get up out of danger. He was the slower of them, although they were each running faster than ever. Guinevere reached for Cedwyn's shoulder, heard a thud, and her hand found only air. He cried out as he hit the ground. The exposed tree root had claimed its first victim of the day.

She reached down to help him up, but his foot was stuck solid. Seeing the boar grow in size as it got closer, Guinevere's brain frantically looked for a way to save Cedwyn and herself. If she made enough noise, she could get the boar to follow her into the forest. That would give Cedwyn time to get loose and up the tree.

"I'll lead the boar away. Get yourself free and then head for that tree." Cedwyn looked in the direction Guinevere pointed. "Get up in it as far as you can go and hang on until I let you know it's safe to come down. All right?"

Cedwyn nodded, his blue eyes wide with fear.

"Stay down and be still 'til you hear from me. Then be quick!"

He nodded again.

Guinevere jumped up and shouted, "Halloo boar! Here I am. Come and get me!" She waved her arms, diverting the boar's attention to her. Once spotted, she ran. The pounding of its hooves told her the boar was following and, if possible, coming even faster. "Cedwyn! Now!" Guinevere shouted, and then she dashed for the safety of the trees.

Behind her, the boar charged, pain fueling its rage. Thundering through the grasses and scrub brush, it focused only on reaching the creature responsible for its pain. Behind them, Cedwyn frantically dug and pulled on the root to free his foot.

"Guin'ver! I can't get loose!"

"You have to! Try harder! Pull harder!"

Cedwyn dug and pulled some more until he felt his foot start to loosen. Finally pulling free, he stood up. He could see the boar charging after Guinevere. He ran for the pine tree. Grabbing branches, he pulled himself up until he was too high for the boar to reach.

"I'm in the tree!" he yelled. Guinevere waved and continued running.

Once in the forest, she stopped to let her eyes adjust to the darkness, and as she waited, the sounds of the boar grew louder. Finally, she could just make out a faint trail. She ran down the path, trying to find some place to hide so that the boar would run past her.

Then up ahead she saw a pine tree with low branches. Finding the last bit of speed inside of her, she reached the tree and jumped. Her hands grasped a low branch, and the pine needles pricked her skin. She pulled herself up, her arms aching from the effort.

Before she could get a good hold, the whole tree shook. Pine needles fell, sticking in her hair and on her clothes. Screaming, she struggled to hold on, ignoring the bark cutting into her skin. *At least if the boar gets me, I won't have my thirteenth Birth Day.* She didn't know which would be worse: the boar or turning thirteen.

The boar charged the tree again. Her grip loosened. She screamed louder, suddenly sure that turning thirteen wouldn't be as bad as facing the angry boar.

"Guin'ver! I'm coming!" Cedwyn's only answer was another scream from the forest. He loosened his arms and slid down the tree, unmindful of the scratches from the bark.

Guinevere's right arm flailed above her, blindly searching for a higher branch. Her fingertips brushed the bottom of one sliding through the sap. She stretched up, grasping the branch firmly with one hand. Trying not to think of what would happen if she fell, she let go with her other hand. For just a moment she felt herself slipping down, but her fingers found the branch, and she held on. The boar hit the tree again. It shook hard enough to nearly topple over, and Guinevere screamed once more.

Then she heard another more horrible scream. Its piercing sound traveled up the trunk into her body. Thinking it was Cedwyn, she looked down and saw a rock hit the boar's side with the arrow. Its angry cry filled the air one last time before the wounded animal ran off deep into the forest.

Guinevere leaned against the rough pine trying to breathe.

"Is it gone? Can you see it?" Cedwyn said as he peeked out

from behind a bush.

Guinevere searched the path that the boar had taken. There was no sign of it, and she couldn't hear it anymore either.

"It's gone. We're safe. C'mon out."

As Cedwyn made his way to her, she climbed down the tree and sat on the ground, her legs too wobbly to hold her. Both of them were a mess. Guinevere proceeded to brush some of the dirt, pine needles, and small twigs off her clothing. Strands of hair had escaped from her braid, and she tried to tuck them back as she pulled out the pine needles. Cedwyn also brushed dirt off his clothes as Guinevere reached over and rubbed some dirt off his cheek. They looked at each other and then burst out laughing from relief at still being alive.

"I..thought..we..were...dead!" Cedwyn said between laughs.

"You should have felt that tree shake! I was sure I was the boar's next meal!" Then Guinevere added, somewhat subdued, "Thank you for coming to my rescue."

"You saved me too. That's what friends are for."

"Yes. I'm only glad that we're still alive to be friends," she said, smiling down at him. "Let's go. We're really late now, and we don't even have a rabbit as a peace offering."

He nodded. "We're gonna be in trouble." Then, as if someone had heard them, upon the wind came a faint but clear voice.

"Lady Guinevere! Cedwyn!"

Grabbing hands, the two ran, fearful of what awaited them at the castle.

Suddenly Cedwyn stopped and pulled Guinevere backwards, almost knocking her down. Grinning, he pointed under a bush at the side of the path. Laughter spilled out from her as she saw their trap in the thicket where they had set it earlier that morning. It was no longer empty. Inside crouched their peace offering: their rabbit! They released the rabbit and put it in a bag, their good humor restored. Then the wind carried the voice again, this time louder and angrier.

"Lady Guinevere! Cedwyn!"

Chapter 2
The Rabbit

Both children stood in the bailey courtyard, still breathing hard from their run back to the castle. Cedwyn's mum Brynwyn stood before them. Her stern look left no doubt that they were in trouble. She glanced from one to the other and shook her head.

"Both of you know better than to be gone all morning and without a proper breakfast," she scolded. "You know you have certain responsibilities, even at your ages." Her gaze burned into Guinevere's brown eyes.

Guinevere lowered her head, ashamed at being in trouble. Cedwyn stood beside her, his eyes on the ground.

"It's too late to eat, so you can both just get busy." She paused, waiting for a protest from them. None came. "Cedwyn, have the courtyard raked by mid-afternoon, or I'll send you to the stable to help," Brynwyn said. Reaching up, her leathered hand pushed strands of black and white hair back into place, and her focus shifted to Guinevere.

"And you, Lady Guinevere, make haste to the schoolroom for your lessons. Both of you should be grateful that your backsides are not sore after being gone!" she added as she turned toward the kitchen, the bag with the rabbit in her hand.

Guinevere started to leave, but Cedwyn didn't move. He was on the verge of tears. Noticing this, she gave him a hug.

"Don't fret, your mum will forget being mad at us by supper time."

"Mayhap, but you don't have to rake the courtyard and maybe even clean the stables."

"No, I just have to spend the next three hours inside that stuffy old schoolroom with Professor Rymes. At least you'll be outside and able to enjoy the rest of the day."

"Wanna trade?"

"No," she said, shaking her head. "The last time we tried that, we both ended up with sore backsides and cleaning the stables too." Grimacing, she stepped inside the doorway to the upper staircase. "I'll see you later."

Slowly, Guinevere made her way up the stone steps in the tower. She didn't like the schoolroom. In the middle of the keep, the room had no windows to let in the air. In the summer it was too hot, and in the winter the stone floor froze her feet like ice. She obediently continued climbing, but her heart weighed her down, threatening to stop her steps before she reached the schoolroom. There at last, she opened the door without knocking.

Professor Rymes stood waiting by the window, his arms crossed, and his right foot tapping the stone floor. The look he gave Guinevere re-enforced the shame she felt with Brynwyn. With his brown cape flowing down over his belted tunic and pants, Rymes looked very imposing, especially with his oversized body.

"It's about time, young lady. Your father is going to hear how you missed an hour today. And that this is not the first time!"

"I'm sorry, Professor," Guinevere said. "I will take care that it doesn't happen again."

"Just be sure you do that. I will not be reprimanded by your father because of your behavior. Now sit down and let's run through your Latin phrases." The professor maneuvered his body into the chair, smoothing his dark brown cape as he sat.

Guinevere sat in the small desk in front of him, conscious of his disapproving eyes as he took in her dirty and damp clothing. Dutifully, she recited the required phrases as he asked for them, but her pronunciation was not exact.

"Have you been practicing on a regular basis?"

"Sometimes."

"Sometimes is not the same as a regular basis. You must practice every night so that your brain does not forget the pronunciation. I've told the king that," Professor Rymes stated. "I'm going to have to request again that he be more involved in your education."

"But it is not interesting. No one else in the castle except for you and my father even speak Latin. There is no one to practice with. I don't understand why I have to learn it," Guinevere said, pouting as she looked Professor Rymes in the eye. Well really, four eyes since he wore glasses.

"I have told you before, Ladies of the Castle need to be able to speak and understand Latin. Since the death of the Queen, there has been no Lady of the Castle. But that will change in a couple of days. It is time for you to step up and assume those duties. And that includes conversing in Latin with high-ranking visitors from abroad."

Guinevere swallowed hard, reminded again that she would be expected to take an adult's role in the castle come her thirteenth Birth Day.

"My father knows Latin. He always uses it when talking to the visiting bishop."

"The king is an exception. Your future husband will most likely be relying on you being able to converse in Latin should such a visitor appear at your castle."

"Ugh! Can we not speak of marriage? After all, I'm not thirteen yet," Guinevere said.

"I am not discussing marriage with you. I am only pointing out the reasons for your education," he explained, removing his glasses and cleaning them on his cape. As he put them back on and adjusted them, he said, "Now, if we may continue with your lessons? Let's do some arithmetic. Where are those sums you were supposed to do?"

Guinevere walked over to the shelf and grabbed some papers

and her charcoal writing tool. Surprisingly, for the next hour, the two worked together eagerly, both enjoying the problems and working the sums.

"Very good," the Professor told her when they were finished. "I just wish you took to Latin as eagerly and quickly as arithmetic. Now, I know it is late but we should touch on the history..."

He was interrupted by the loud rumbling of Guinevere's stomach. She quickly put one hand on her stomach and tried to hide her grin with the other.

"I must say, that is not very ladylike, is it?" he said, removing his glasses again and cleaning them on his cape.

"I'm sorry, Professor. Cedwyn and I missed breakfast this morning, and there was not time to grab something from the kitchen," Guinevere apologized.

"That should teach you to go traipsing about. Lucky for you and the castle those days are coming to an end. But we'll stop for now. You need to go to the kitchen and help with the cooking. Mayhap that will go better for you than Latin. I will see you tomorrow, on time." His stare stifled any reply. "And don't forget to eat so you don't sample everything you help prepare."

"Thank you, Professor Rymes," Guinevere replied. Grumbling, she made her way down the stairs. "I don't want my traipsing about days to come to an end. If only there was some way to postpone my Birth Day or make Father realize I'm not ready to be the Lady of the Castle."

Concerned with her problems, she nearly missed Cedwyn on the stone steps outside the kitchen. His mouth full of bread and cheese, he grabbed her tunic and motioned to the cloth beside him. She sat down and unwrapped it, revealing pieces of bread and cheese inside. She dove into the food hungrily. They stopped only to drink the sweet aleberry cider from the amphora cup.

When she finished, she turned to Cedwyn. "That was the best food I have eaten in a long time."

"Me too. Since last night!" Cedwyn said somewhat accusingly. "Mum decided I had to help clean the stables after all. And, she said that since I had already waited so long to eat, a couple more hours wouldn't hurt. I think she was trying to make a point."

Guinevere looked contrite. "I'm sorry. I never meant to be gone so long this morning. If it weren't for that bloody boar, we would have been home sooner. Thanks for saving me some food. Professor Rymes wouldn't let me eat either."

"Are you going inside to help?" Cedwyn motioned behind him to the entrance of the kitchen.

"Yes. All ladies need to know how to cook. Just once I would like for Father to ask me what I want to know," Guinevere said, smoothing her tunic where it had dried from the morning dew.

"And what do you want to know?"

"I don't know. Mayhap how to catch a horse, shoot a crossbow, hunt a deer," she replied. "Something adventurous. But, I best be getting in the kitchen. I'll be in enough trouble once the professor tells Father I was late and didn't know my Latin. I can at least learn how to cook a good supper."

Guinevere tousled Cedwyn's hair and walked up the steps.

Cedwyn skipped across the inner courtyard leaving small dust plumes behind him, his good mood back. Finding the best place to sit on the drawbridge, he peered intently into the slow moving water of the moat. After supper, he would give Guinevere a full report on the numerous creatures swimming in there.

Guinevere wrinkled up her nose at the smell of raw meat and blood mixed with fresh herbs that floated out of the kitchen door. It always smelled better when they baked bread in the early morning. By mid-afternoon, the rich aroma had faded. Instead the air smelled of pigs, horses, cows, and chickens. The breeze that flowed through the slats in the outer wall and circulated around the bailey courtyard barely made the kitchen bearable in the afternoon.

The kitchen was a hub of activity. From a side alcove, the blackguard Edward, a tall skinny boy around fifteen, was setting out the pots and utensils that would be used to prepare supper. His freckled face bore spots of charcoal on it from the soot-covered pots.

In the back, the carver James sharpened the last of the knives on the whetstone. Older than Edward by three years, his arms bulged with muscle gained from sharpening knives and cutting meat. His leather apron was stained with blood.

In the middle of the bare dirt floor stood a large black caldron on a bed of pine and hickory wood. Small wisps of flame still licked at the remaining sticks of wood. Guinevere breathed in the wood smoke, savoring its smell. Off to the side, smaller caldrons also simmered on similar beds of pine and hickory.

Several women stood talking around the different caldrons. Some added sprigs of thyme and parsley while others measured out chopped onions and mushrooms to be added later. Brynwyn, Cedwyn's mum, moved among the caldrons, stopping to taste and have additional seasonings added. Her grey-streaked hair was now pulled back in a bun. A pale brown apron covered with samplings of previous dinners covered her ankle-length dress. While she was in charge of the kitchen, she only interfered in Cook's domain when a big feast was planned. She seemed to sense Guinevere's presence.

"Lady Guinevere, don't just stand there. Your father is having important guests tonight for supper," Brynwyn said, resting her hands on her stout hips.

"I didn't know," Guinevere said.

"He is, and there is much to do. Help Maggie with the potatoes and the carrots." She pointed to a girl close to Guinevere's age busy peeling vegetables. Maggie looked up from her work, but showed no other sign that she knew Guinevere.

"The lot needs to be peeled and cut up to put in the pot here. Goin' to be a real nice supper. Plenty of vegetables and pork in garlic and pepper sauce, bread, and plenty of ale. Oh, and I almost forgot. Cook is making a special dish out of a barnacle goose and that rabbit you and Cedwyn brought in. That may save you a bit of trouble with your father," she added, turning back to the pot she was tasting.

"I hope so. Is Cook by any chance baking circlette?" Guinevere asked, her mouth watering just thinking of the almond cake topped with fresh raspberry jam.

Brynwyn turned, a slight smile forming on her weathered face. "Yes, he is. So you best stay on his good side this time. No accidents today. He can't be making proper circlette if he has to work around a mess like the last time. Behave yourself and be careful."

Guinevere nodded. Maggie looked shyly at Guinevere and motioned toward the knives used for peeling. She thanked her, but the older girl didn't reply. Guinevere just shrugged and started peeling a potato. Maggie was a plain girl with her mouse-brown hair tied up in a bun like Brynwyn's. Like most of the girls in the castle, her clothes consisted of a well-worn tunic with no design. She also wore no shoes.

Maggie never talked to anyone that Guinevere knew. In fact, it had taken months just to get a nod out of Maggie when she started working in the kitchen. But Guinevere didn't mind. She always told Maggie about everything she and Cedwyn had been doing. Once in a while, she even managed to get a smile out of Maggie, although she was careful not to let the other girl know that she saw it.

After an hour, the pile of peeled potatoes and carrots had grown. Maggie had long ago stopped peeling and had been cutting up the vegetables. After finishing her pile of potatoes, Guinevere went in search of a pan to put them in. As she was coming back with the pan, Cook called out to her.

"Lady Guinevere, if it is possible without causing a riot, bring me that wicker basket with the rabbit in it. And don't open it!" he added, wiping his hands on his stained apron. His arms, heavily muscled from years of kneading dough, looked as if they could easily squeeze the life out of a child if given a reason.

"Yes, Cook," Guinevere said, not wanting to risk his wrath. She put the pan down by Maggie and went to get the basket.

While not heavy, she sensed movement inside. The rabbit was still alive. That would mean that she would have to watch as Cook killed and skinned it. Guinevere shivered and walked over to the other side of the kitchen where Cook waited.

Apparently, though, the rabbit knew what was in store and had no intention of being part of supper that night. And it didn't care who got in trouble.

The basket jumped out of Guinevere's hands before she could even blink. Hitting the floor, the lid came off and the rabbit, seeing its opportunity, ran across the kitchen. Guinevere just stood there, stunned. Maggie leaped up from her stool screaming as the rabbit

15

dove under her legs. The pan she was filling with vegetables flew into the air, carrots and potatoes going all over. Brynwyn shouted for James to block the doorway. Cook bore down on Guinevere, murder in his eyes.

"I only did what I was told! The rabbit jumped in the basket, and it slipped! It wasn't my fault!"

"You just wait until I tell the king about this...this fiasco!" Cook shouted, his plump face turning as red as the potatoes she'd peeled.

Guinevere turned and ran to the back of the kitchen, looking under the shelves for the rabbit. She had to catch it. That was the only way to avoid trouble. Her father would be furious with her for wreaking havoc once again in the kitchen.

"It's over here!" Edward yelled as he exited the alcove with additional pans and utensils. The rabbit darted out of the alcove and dashed for the door. Running to cut the rabbit off, Cook collided with Edward who was also trying to block the doorway. Pans and utensils flew into the air. Cook pounced too late on the rabbit which turned and raced for the back of the kitchen.

"There it goes! It's heading for the drainage pipe!" The pipe drained the kitchen when it was washed down to the packed earth once a month. It came out at the edge of the woods.

Guinevere hurried to the far end of the kitchen. There, indeed heading for the drain pipe, the only way left unguarded, was the rabbit. It raced toward the pipe as if its continued existence depended upon making it. Which it did.

Knowing that she could not reach the pipe before the rabbit, Guinevere sped out the door, bent on reaching the end of the pipe before the rabbit.

Already alerted to a problem from the yells and screams coming from the kitchen, the bailey courtyard was rapidly filling up with spectators. The blacksmith Sauder, his hair and face stained with soot, just shook his head as Guinevere flew past. Several others, including the stable boys and gardeners, stopped their work to watch, and ventured out of the castle gates to see what else was happening. Several ladies in various stages of cleaning the castle hung out of the upper windows and hollered down as she passed.

"What have you done now, Lady Guinevere?"

"Why are you running? What have you done?"

Guinevere ignored their questions and concentrated on where she was going. She ran to the gate at the edge of the inner courtyard and out onto the bridge. She rushed passed Cedwyn so swiftly that she didn't even see him, focused as she was on the rabbit.

"I've got to get there first," she stressed to herself.

"Wait a minute! What's goin' on? Where you goin'?" Cedwyn yelled. Receiving no response, he abandoned his moat watching and sprinted after her, still shouting.

Several others also followed, though keeping at a safe distance. No one wanted to be close when the king arrived, as he was sure to do with all the ruckus. Some had found out the hard way that when Lady Guinevere got in trouble, those close by were usually on the receiving end of the king's anger also. In fact, sometimes he directed his anger at those milling around rather than at Guinevere.

Guinevere ran on, her breath coming in gasps, but she didn't slow down. She could see the tall grass where the pipe spilled out its rotten treasure once a month. *I'm going to make it. Yes!* She silently cheered. On she ran, her eyes glued on the spot.

By this time, quite a crowd had gathered and followed her out the castle gate, over the moat, and across the meadow. Many of the women shook their heads as they watched Lady Guinevere tear across the meadow in a very unladylike way. Children of all sizes raced past the women, their cheers echoing alongside Cedwyn's repeated demands of what she was doing. Several men folk, including the blacksmith Sauder and Professor Rymes, drawn away from their work by the pursuing crowds and shouts, followed.

Focused as she was, Guinevere didn't see what was coming through the clearing. She didn't hear Cedwyn's shouts of warning, joined by the shouts of the rest of the spectators.

She did see the grass at the pipe's end begin to flatten as if the winter wind were blowing in a storm. The rabbit was coming out of the pipe! Guinevere ran harder. She had to catch that rabbit.

From nowhere a blur of fur streaked toward the pipe, almost knocking her down. The odor of wet dog assailed her senses, and its howling as it spotted the rabbit echoed in her ears. Not knowing where the bratchet dog came from, only knowing that it was after her rabbit, Guinevere yelled and ran even faster.

"No! The rabbit's mine!"

It was a race to the end! Guinevere's salvation or the bratchet's supper!

Dimly in the far reaches of her mind, Guinevere recognized the terrified voices of Cedwyn and the others. But she did not waver. Then Cedwyn's cries grew more desperate and more terrified.

"Guin'ver! Look out! Guin'ver!"

Without stopping, she looked around, hoping she would not stumble. Her ears rang with the bratchet's howling that was growing louder as it sensed victory was close.

She glimpsed a huge dark form barreling down on her from the forest road like a granite chip down a slope, picking up speed with no chance of stopping. Fear worked its way into her mind.

"What...?"

She became conscious of Cedwyn's frantic shouting. The roars of the others also filtered into her brain.

"Guin'ver! Look out! Guin'ver!"

"Lady Guinevere!"

"Look out, my Lady!"

"Oh, my!"

The towering form materialized into the shape of a galloping horse with a knight dressed in shining silver armor. He raced straight toward her as if she were his opponent in a jousting competition. Paralyzing fear stopped her. She could only watch as knight and horse bore down on her as if she weren't there.

Sir Pellinore saw the girl and the danger, but he couldn't swerve around her. He was also focused, focused on his bratchet that was now off on another trail. So quickly was the Painted Dragon forgotten in the face of more convenient prey!

Powerless to move, Guinevere also found herself unable to scream. Then, without warning, she left the ground. The rush of wind from Pellinore's passing whipped around her even as she moved through the air. With a thwack, she landed on the ground, the wind knocked out of her.

In the few moments she struggled to breathe, Guinevere became aware of an apparition in flowing grey robes and a long white beard standing beside her. A frown of disapproval covered the wrinkled face.

"Wa... wai..."

"Fine behavior for the future Queen of England," the apparition said before striding away. The rest of the crowd started to retreat to the castle as word filtered down that Lady Guinevere was safe.

CHAPTER 3
THE MEETING

"Wait!" Guinevere cried as she gingerly struggled to her feet, still fighting to breathe. Tears made their way down her face leaving streaks in the dirt that coated her. Her hands went to her backside, still stinging from the landing.

The apparition continued toward the castle, but stopped to pat Cedwyn on the head. The boy responded with a huge smile.

"Merlyn. Please wait!" Guinevere hurried as fast as she could to where he and Cedwyn stood, unmindful of the quietly dispersing crowd.

"Yes, Lady Guinevere?" Merlyn replied, a slight smile tugging at his lips, but one that Guinevere did not see.

"Thank you," she murmured.

"You are quite welcome. Now let's try to act a little bit more like a lady, shall we?"

"Yes, Merlyn," she said. "But who was that, and why did you call me the future Queen of England?"

"Yes, who was that knight, Merlyn?" Cedwyn chimed in, tugging at Merlyn's robe. "And Guin'ver, what were you chasing? I never saw anything come out of the castle. Are you going to do magic, Merlyn? Can we watch?"

"Hold on," Merlyn said with a chuckle. "Hold on. Only one question at a time!"

"Who was that knight?" both children asked in unison.

Merlyn laughed and pointed toward the forest. "That was Sir Pellinore. Quite a knight in his day, although some now say that he is, well, a bit eccentric."

"What's *ec'ent'ic*?" Cedwyn interrupted.

"That means some people think that he's crazy, while others think that he's bewitched."

"Can't you unb'witch him?" Cedwyn asked.

"No, I cannot." He held up his hand to stop further questions. "Sir Pellinore is bewitched by himself. And that I cannot undo."

"What do you mean?" Guinevere asked.

"For many years now, Sir Pellinore has been obsessed with a strange creature that some say is magical itself. He has been chasing the Painted Dragon with that bratchet hound of his for a long time."

"What is the Painted Dragon?" Guinevere asked.

"Just your typical dragon except for one thing." They waited. "It looks like someone just threw buckets of paint all over it. Must be four or five different colors. Yellow, black, green, red, and something else. Never seen another one like it."

Merlyn paused to scratch his chin under his beard.

"Nothing moves Pellinore far from the dragon's path. Nothing, that is, except when the bratchet finds another trail, or Pellinore sees something beautiful like a maiden or a unicorn, or he comes across a jousting match. But even then his attention is drawn away only briefly. Then they are off and hunting again. Some say it is the Painted Dragon that has bewitched him, but I doubt it. Anyway, I think that Sir Pellinore would find his life rather dull if there was no Painted Dragon to hunt."

"What happens when he catches this dragon?" Cedwyn asked.

"I'm not sure. It just might be the end of Sir Pellinore. After all, he would have no further quest."

"That would be sad."

Cedwyn nodded his agreement.

"The next question is ours," Merlyn said to Guinevere.

"Yes, Guin'ver. What were you after?" Cedwyn asked.

"The rabbit."

"The rabbit?" Merlyn echoed.

"Yes, the rabbit that Cedwyn and I caught this morning. Cook asked me to bring it to him so he could fix it for dinner. It jumped out of the basket and took off," she explained. "Now I am really going to be in trouble. The last time I had to help in the kitchen things didn't go well either. This is not turning into a good day."

Cedwyn interrupted. "Is that what the bratchet was after?"

"I imagine it was," Merlyn replied.

"We still have other questions, right Merlyn?" Cedwyn asked.

"Yes, we..." Merlyn did not finish as he saw an anxious look come over Guinevere's face.

"And now it has just gotten worse."

He turned to follow her gaze.

There, striding through the castle gates, was the daunting figure of King Leodegrance, Guinevere's father. Clad in a simple grey shirt with his black pants tucked into his knee-high boots, the King exuded grace and power. And from the rigid set of his shoulders and the determined look on his face, Guinevere knew he had heard of her mishaps during the day. She was in trouble.

The broad plain outside the castle walls was deserted except for the three of them and her father. Everyone else had long since disappeared so as not to be on the receiving end of any of the king's anger. Also, they did not enjoy seeing Lady Guinevere get into trouble. True, she caused most of her predicaments with her mischievousness, but the subjects of King Leodegrance liked Lady Guinevere.

"Your Highness," Merlyn greeted the king, removing his pointed grey hat and bowing his head while sending the king a wink. With the two men at the same height, neither had any trouble looking the other in the eye. King Leodegrance acknowledged Merlyn's wink with a barely perceptible nod.

"Cedwyn, your mother is looking for help to clean up the kitchen. Please go and see her."

Cedwyn shuddered and glanced at Guinevere as he bowed to

the king.

"Don't you worry about Guinevere, young Cedwyn. I imagine that tomorrow the two of you will find another adventure to go on or more mischief to get into. Now, run along so your mother is not kept waiting."

"Yes, Your Highness," Cedwyn replied. Then with a quick smile at Merlyn and a last sympathetic glance at Guinevere, he ran over the drawbridge and through the castle gate.

"Well, Lady Guinevere. Need I say that once again I have received numerous reports on your behavior?"

Guinevere raised her eyes from the ground and looked at her father, dread filling her heart. She opened her mouth to reply, but stopped when the king held up his hand.

"I have warned you and Cedwyn about venturing out into the forest by yourselves and about being gone so long. Brynwyn said it was half past the morning when the two of you finally showed up."

"Yes, but we brought back a rabbit for supper," Guinevere said, knowing that her father had forbidden her to talk yet.

"Did you? And where may I ask is that rabbit now? Cook does not appear to have it and neither do you."

"It got away when I was bringing it to Cook. I was trying to get it back when Sir Pellinore and his dog and Merlyn appeared," Guinevere said, trying to defend herself.

"Ah, yes. It is a good thing Merlyn did appear, is it not?"

Guinevere nodded.

"Because if Merlyn had not appeared, then it is quite possible that the conversation we are having now would not be taking place. Right?"

Guinevere nodded again.

"Because you probably would not be here but out there, trampled and bleeding on the ground. Trampled because you became so caught up in your circumstances that you forgot your surroundings, that you forgot you might be putting yourself in danger, so caught up in your circumstances that you forgot you are supposed to be acting like the king's daughter, not his son!" King Leodegrance finished quietly but sternly, running a hand through his black and grey hair.

"I'm sorry, Father. I do not mean to cause you so much trouble," Guinevere said, tears of shame at disappointing her father filling her eyes.

"Guinevere, it is not the trouble that you do not mean that causes me such anxiety. It is the trouble that you may end up causing the entire castle if you continue to act without thought. Perhaps while Merlyn is here, he may have some influence on that. Now get to your room. Brynwyn has already sent a lady to help you get dressed for supper. The rest of our guests are already starting to arrive."

Guinevere looked behind her. Numerous horses, riders, and wagons were moving along the forest road a half mile down from the castle. The late afternoon sun glinted off the knights' armor and the horses' harnesses and bridles. She could faintly make out the squeaking of the wagon wheels.

"Yes, Father. I will try hard to be good," Guinevere said, head down, as she turned to leave.

"Guinevere."

"Yes?"

"You are good. But it's time for you to be more ladylike so people will see you as the Lady of the Castle now, not as a mischievous child," her father finished as his hand brushed her brown hair away from her face.

Guinevere nodded and walked away. As she prepared to cross the drawbridge, her father called out to her.

"Don't think that I have forgotten about missing an hour of your schooling or not practicing your Latin!"

"No, Father," she replied, quickening her pace.

King Leodegrance sighed as he turned toward Merlyn.

"Welcome, my old friend. Maybe while you are here you can assist with the raising of my daughter! The young lady needs a woman's touch, not the hardened hand of a warrior."

"But she has the love of that warrior and that is what is important, King Leodegrance."

"That may be, but at times like now, I wish desperately for her mother's touch. She had such a way with people, even hardened warriors," the king added.

"I take it that Lady Guinevere does not know the significance of tonight's supper feast and the guests."

"I know that she seems to be balking at her approaching duties, but... No! Wait! What do you mean? I didn't even know I was having guests until Arthur arrived a couple of hours ago!" The king eyed Merlyn. "How did you know I was having guests?"

Merlyn smiled.

"Darn it, Merlyn! Why can't you live in the present like the rest of us?"

"Now that would offer no challenge," Merlyn countered. "Well, not to worry. Things will work out for the best. They always do. And I will have a talk with her while I'm here. Despite everything that has happened, she is an obedient child, and she is your daughter. I imagine that she will do the right thing when the time comes," Merlyn finished.

King Leodegrance nodded his head, confusion still showing on his face. "I hope so, I think. But my, our guests come nearer. We had better get ready to receive them."

Guinevere leaned out on the window sill, having finally reached her destination. When she had started getting dressed, she had been on the other side of her bedroom.

Similar to the other bedrooms in the keep, hers contained only a minimum of furniture. She had her bed, a table and chair for doing her studying, and a trunk for her clothes. The one difference sat in the middle of the room. A handmade rug rich with bright greens, purples, blues, and reds covered most of the floor. It was a present from her father on his return from a long trip several years ago. And while the colors had started to fade like spring flowers in summer, Guinevere still loved getting out of bed and standing on the rug instead of the cold stone floor in the winter.

"Lady Guinevere! If you don't keep still I can't get your smock fixed right."

"But it's so exciting, Mary. We haven't had so many guests since last summer. And they are still coming!" Guinevere said as she leaned out the window. The entire bailey blazed with torches. People were walking back and forth talking and laughing.

26

Mary moved next to her. "Yes, it is exciting, isn't it!"

Guinevere was surprised to realize that Mary was just as thrilled by the visitors. Although only three years separated the girls, they did not spend that much time together. Mary usually came to help Guinevere dress for special occasions or to help her pack when she and the king went to visit other castles on business.

"Momma says that there is a good chance that I may be chosen tonight for marriage to one of the knights."

"Really?"

"Oh, yes, my Lady. And I am so thrilled. Just imagine having one of those men to look after and to have him care for me."

Guinevere then realized that the age difference between them was greater than just the three years Mary had on her. Unlike Guinevere, Mary glowed with the possibility of marriage. Her coal black eyes sparkled, and her straight black hair shined. Small yellow flowers were woven through her locks. Her light brown smock was decorated with green embroidery and small silver bells. *She does look ready to be married*, Guinevere thought. *Thank goodness it won't be me.*

"Why, there might even be a prospect for you, my Lady, out there tonight. Mayhap some high-ranking knight or even a neighboring king's son will fall deeply in love with you," Mary continued, getting into the spirit. "Then, in several months, he will come back again and ask your father for your hand in marriage."

"My father would never let that happen. I'm too young to even think of marriage. I'm only going to be thirteen. Besides, Father didn't even say anything about tonight until right before I came up to get dressed," Guinevere protested.

"You're probably right, my Lady," she said. "But let's make sure that you look nice anyway." Mary finished adorning Guinevere's forest green smock with tiny silver bells and a white embroidered sash. "Now, hold still, Lady Guinevere. I need to fix your hair."

She brushed Guinevere's brown hair until it shined. As a finishing touch, Mary tied the hair back at the nape of her neck with a strip of dark brown rawhide and then wove green ivy throughout.

"There you are, my Lady," Mary said, stepping back to admire her work.

Guinevere moved over to her mum's mirror. She gasped as she glimpsed the young lady looking back at her. This was not the Guinevere from the forest that morning with dew dripping off her tunic and twigs tangled in her hair. Looking back at her was the image of her mother that she kept locked in her heart.

"Oh my," she whispered, tears filling her eyes. "This is supposed to be me in two days." She shook her head. "I don't want to be the Lady of the Castle."

"My Lady?"

Guinevere kept her eyes averted as she turned to leave. "Nothing. Thank you, Mary."

"I bet Cedwyn won't recognize you." Mary laughed and followed Guinevere down the stairs.

As they approached the Great Hall, the din grew louder. Voices laughed, talked, and even argued good-naturedly. Cedwyn stood on a bench at the edge of the doorway peering into the hall. Guinevere eased up beside him as Mary went inside.

"Seen anything interesting?" she asked and steadied Cedwyn as he wobbled on the bench.

"Guin'ver! Don't be sneaking up on me like that. I almost fell!" Then he looked at her again. "You look different tonight. Like you're growed up."

"I know."

"What's the matter?"

"Nothing. I'm just not sure... Mary seems to think that this is a special night."

"It must be." Cedwyn's attention was drawn back to the hall. "Look at all those knights, real knights in there! See? And look at all the armor and weapons!" He pointed. Various types of armor from chain mail to solid metal stood against the wall. Swords, mallets, and other weapons lay in front, ready to grab should an attack occur.

Guinevere looked in and marveled at the people and all the activity. The smoke from the torches spiraled up to the vents in the ceiling. The flames of the fires flickered as when the night breeze brushed the campfire as people found their places for supper. Indeed, there were many knights. Their deep voices were the ones Guinevere had heard as she approached.

Row upon row of knights lined the long tables that spanned the length of the hall. Standards were abundant also. Every order of knights had its own standard, the banner of their king they carried into battle. These were displayed behind them, so no one would question their loyalty. Guinevere found that she knew several. The striking red snake on a coal black background symbolized King Peredur. The crouching lion symbolized King Landamur of the southernmost country. In the far corner stood the mighty bear symbol of King Anewyn, and next to it, the fighting dragons.

"Who belongs to the fighting dragons?"

"I saw the knights come in with it, but I don't know the king that carries it. But I do know where he is. He's sitting with your father and Merlyn," Cedwyn replied.

Guinevere looked toward the front of the Great Hall. At the massive table signifying her father's stature sat a number of men. In the middle her father sat with Merlyn on one side and the unknown king on the other side. Though not old like her father, the scar on his left cheek testified to hard times. His black tunic, adorned with a red sash, bore the fighting dragons. He and her father appeared deep in conversation.

"I don't know him either," she said.

Then, as if by magic, Merlyn appeared by their sides.

"Lady Guinevere. I must say you look so like your mother. She would be proud of you."

She swallowed hard, trying to hold back the tears his words brought. "Thank you," she murmured, pausing before raising her eyes to meet Merlyn's.

He smiled at her and touched her shoulder. "Proud of you, yes sir."

Merlyn then motioned toward the door. "Supper is ready to be served. Cedwyn, the king has requested that you sit at the right end of his table as Lady Guinevere's guest."

Both children looked stunned.

"That's right. No kitchen tonight. King Leodegrance thought it was time for Lady Guinevere to participate in a feast since her thirteenth Birth Day is the day after tomorrow. And you, Cedwyn, have the honor of keeping her company. Just see that the two of you cause no mischief. The king would be displeased if that were to be the case," Merlyn warned.

"Who is that man sitting on the other side of Father?"

"That, Lady, is King Arthur, king of the eastern and southern borders. He has only attained his kingship recently upon the death of his father, Uther Pendragon. He is young, but he is strong and influential and will make an important ally for your father," he informed them. "Now take your places at the table so you are not in the way of the servers."

As Guinevere and Cedwyn made their way to the end of the king's table, her curiosity overrode her misgivings of her approaching Birth Day. King Leodegrance acknowledged their presence with a wave of his hand. His eyes lingered on her, and she sensed his approval of how she looked. He then spoke to King Arthur who also smiled and waved at them.

Guinevere was surprised that King Arthur appeared even younger when he smiled. The action softened the jagged scar on his cheek and his dark eyes sparkled. She and Cedwyn returned both greetings with cheerful waves. They settled down as the servers, including James and Edward, paraded through the tables carrying steaming pots heaped with marinated fowl, turkey, and beef. Guinevere inhaled the garlic and pepper sauce marinade, and her stomach grumbled at the scent. Cedwyn grinned.

Once served, the noise in the hall quieted down. The only sounds echoing throughout the room were the scraping of pots and the setting down of half empty ale cups. The food and drink were plentiful and good, and no one wanted any to go to waste.

She and Cedwyn ate hungrily as well, washing their food down with aleberry, the fruity and spicy drink. It was their favorite and one that was in abundance at feasts.

"I don't think I can eat another bite," Cedwyn said, rubbing his stomach.

"Me either. Everything was good. And you know what?" she

asked. Cedwyn shook his head. "No one even missed the rabbit!" she added, laughing.

Cedwyn joined in and soon they were laughing so hard that they almost disrupted the entire table. However, a stern look from the king quieted both of them; at least it looked so from a distance. They both continued to giggle, but were careful to hide their giggles behind their hands. Several times during dinner, Guinevere caught King Arthur glancing her way, and she gave him bright smiles in return.

"Look," Guinevere said, pointing toward the doorway from the kitchen where Cook led the servers with platters of dessert.

"Oh boy! Circlette!" Cedwyn said. "I was afraid they weren't gonna have any tonight."

"Me too after this afternoon. This is my favorite part of feasts. I love the small cakes with raspberry jam dripping down the sides," Guinevere said.

"I like the almonds and currants inside the best," Cedwyn added.

Although both had eaten until they were so stuffed that it was hard to move, they managed to find room for dessert. The best part of the circlette was licking the sticky raspberry jam from their fingers. They ignored the wash bowl provided until the end, determined to lick every bit of jam from their hands.

Once the serving staff cleared the dishes, the knights started pounding on the tables. Guinevere and Cedwyn covered their ears as the vibrations of the tin cups striking the wooden tables echoed throughout the cavernous hall. When the king stood, the noise grew its loudest and then died down.

As King Leodegrance addressed the assembly before him, Guinevere noticed that he had traded his plain shirt for a black leather one. He spoke of the good times of peace and the need for loyalty from all. He talked of the need to keep alliances even in the face of peaceful times. He talked of the hard road ahead to keep peace throughout the land. Important words for many people. His speech, however, lulled Guinevere and Cedwyn closer to sleep as their full bellies, not their minds, ruled their bodies.

When he finished, the knights took up their cups again and

once more reverberations from the pounding on the tables filled the air. Rousted from their brief nap, Guinevere and Cedwyn joined in with their cups, although not as loudly as the others.

Gradually the din died down, and a general shout filled the air with the arrival of the bard. Even Guinevere and Cedwyn shouted loudly at his approach. The bard always told such magnificent stories. Both children were eager to hear the stories tonight for the first time from inside the room. In the past, they were sent to bed and only managed to hear them by perching under a window outside.

An old man who traveled from village to village and castle to castle, the bard needed two knights to assist him up onto one of the tables in the middle of the hall. He tottered there on shaky legs like a newborn fawn for a few moments. Once steady, he shed his dark cloak adorned with stars and half moons and took his lyre out of a canvas bag. As he strummed, he started his story.

"Long ago after hundreds of years of waiting, an old wizard finally fell in love with a young girl. Unbeknownst to the wizard, however, the beautiful girl bewitched him so that he would fall in love with her."

This part was greeted with boos from the knights.

"Their love affair lasted for many years, and all during that time, the young girl continued to trick the wizard so that he would teach her his magic. Friends of the wizard tried to show him what was happening, but he did not see. He was blinded by his devotion to her."

At this, several areas around the hall erupted in groans and laughter. Some knights, enamored like the wizard, knew what heartache was in store for him. Others, untouched by love so far, shook their heads at the wizard's weakness.

"Eventually, this young maiden had total control over the wizard. And, when he had taught her all his magic, she lured him into a cave with the promise of a surprise. Once inside, she bound him to the wall of the cave and then left him there, buried inside for all eternity."

Many of the knights shook their heads at this. Others, including Guinevere and Cedwyn, murmured their disbelief.

"Thus," said the bard, "it is necessary to watch all alliances with care in case some of you are bewitched by a young maiden's smile!" The bard finished, and the knights pounded on the tables once again to show their approval of the story. As the bard left the hall, the servers returned, this time with great quantities of ale.

A hand closed over Guinevere's shoulder, and she smiled as she saw Merlyn.

"Merlyn, that was such a sad story. Do you think it might be true?" she asked the old wizard.

"I doubt very much whether that insolent old man has ever told a true story in his life," Merlyn replied.

"Well, I liked it," Cedwyn added. "I just wish there would have been magic used, like on animals and trees."

"Another time. But for now, King Leodegrance has requested that you both be dismissed. What happens here now is not for young ones to see. Guinevere, be sure to say good night to your father. Cedwyn, you come with me. I need you to help me talk your mum into stealing some of that circlette for my journey in a couple of days. Good night, Lady Guinevere," Merlyn said, bowing slightly.

"Night Guin'ver," Cedwyn added.

Guinevere walked to her father and put her hand on his shoulder. At her touch he turned and smiled.

"Guinevere, you look just like your mother did at your age."

Her heart threatened to burst at the look of love and pride on his face.

"But, time to call an end to the evening, is it?" She nodded. "Well, I hope you and Cedwyn enjoyed yourselves."

"We did, Father, and thank you for allowing us entrance to the hall this evening."

"Before you go, Guinevere, I would like you to say hello to King Arthur."

At the mention of his name, Arthur stood. Although he towered a good foot and a half above her, his smile made him appear less intimidating. And it did soften the harsh scar on his face. He bent and took her right hand in his and touched his lips to the back of her hand. Guinevere shivered at the touch.

"Lady Guinevere, you do look lovely," he said in a strong husky voice. "It is my pleasure to finally meet you. I have heard much about you this day."

Guinevere blushed, uncertain how to take his compliment and afraid of what he had heard. "Thank you, King Arthur. I hope you are able to come again and bring such entertainment as your coming has brought tonight." She turned then and kissed her father's cheek, his grey beard tickling her nose. "Goodnight, Father."

At the door, she looked back and caught Arthur's eye on her. He smiled again, and flustered, Guinevere nodded slightly before hurrying out.

She stopped by the kitchen to see if she could find Cedwyn and Merlyn. The only ones there were the servants cleaning up after the feast. Continuing across to the keep tower, she mounted the stairs to her room. Her steps were light even though it was late. Visions of Arthur's smile played through her mind, and the excitement of the evening threatened to forestall sleep.

She stopped halfway up and looked out of a window. For several minutes she stared at the numerous fires that signified the many different camps. At times the light of the fires flickered when someone passed in front, bringing a temporary blackness to the field. Breathing deeply, she inhaled the smell of wood smoke and damp grasses, pleasant smells for one raised in the country.

As she moved away from the window, something at the edge of the firelight caught her eye. She paused and looked harder, trying to separate the varied shadows in the distance. There--a slight movement against the dark. Whatever it was, it moved with stealth into the forest, a secret unwilling to be shared. Guinevere hesitated but a moment and then went back down the stairs.

CHAPTER 4
THE SURPRISE

A t the bottom of the stairs, Guinevere paused and peeked out the door. Seeing no one, she stepped out into the bailey, thankful for the clouds that hid the moon. Focused on the outer door across the courtyard, she missed seeing the figure that slid out of the shadows and followed her.

Guinevere glanced once more around the bailey as she reached the outer door. The shadow following her hugged the building as the moon drifted out from the clouds. She crept through the door and turned to the right. Keeping in the shadows and close to the stable wall, she managed to work her way to about twenty yards from the edge of the forest. Taking a furtive look around, she stole across the open grass and slipped into the trees.

As she disappeared from view, the figure following her moved through the outer door. As Guinevere had done, this figure kept close to the stable wall, staying within the shadows and watching the tree line for any movement. Seeing nothing, the shadowy figure moved out into the moonlight, revealing himself to any who happened to be watching, but there were none. Those not in bed stayed in the hall enjoying themselves too much to venture out into the late night. The moonlight bounced off his grey gown and illuminated his white hair, making it appear ghostly. Merlyn quickened his pace, not wanting to fall too far behind.

Guinevere crept along the forest path. The fragrance of wet pine filled her senses. Suddenly, the faint sound of a voice off to her right reached her ears. She turned and moved cautiously through the trees and brush. The calming quality of the voice dispelled her fears. As she moved closer, the voice's volume increased very little. Whoever it belonged to continued to whisper to someone, although Guinevere heard only the one voice.

Through the leafy oak branches, Guinevere made out the shape of a tall, slender woman dressed in a white hooded robe. Edging closer she saw that the woman stood in a small clearing. Moonlight filtered down, descending almost like a halo around her. With the woman's hood up, Guinevere was unable to discern any other physical features. The woman continued to talk to someone concealed by her body. Intrigued, Guinevere moved closer, careful not to make any noise. While the woman did not move, from time to time her arms reached out in front of her, for some reason unknown to Guinevere.

So absorbed by the sight in front of her, Guinevere didn't sense Merlyn moving up behind her. Stopping about five paces away, he also watched with a sense of fascination and relief. The woman's slender arms reached up and removed her hood, revealing lush, curly, brown hair that fell lightly upon her shoulders.

Merlyn moved closer to Guinevere. As the woman knelt down holding her hands out in front of her, Merlyn silently and swiftly put his left hand on Guinevere's left shoulder. At the same time he covered her mouth, effectively silencing her gasp when Guinevere saw the unicorn.

"Shh. It's Merlyn. We need to be quiet so we don't frighten it. Understand?"

Guinevere nodded, and Merlyn removed his hand from her mouth, but still left his hand on her shoulder to restrain her from moving forward.

"I've never seen anything so beautiful and so pure," she whispered, her brown eyes sparkling in the dim moonlight and dancing with excitement.

"And you probably never will again. Unicorns are rare and almost never seen by regular people."

Guinevere's eyes drank in the pure white beauty of the unicorn. Its coat glistened in the moonlight. Long, soft, and cloud-white were the only words to describe the creature's mane and tail. As she watched, the unicorn regally bowed its horned head and let the woman scratch around its ears. The horn shined like it had been polished, its brilliant bone color blinding when the moonlight caught it right.

A shift in the wind alerted the unicorn to the presence of the strangers. Tensing and raising its head, the unicorn backed up a few steps, its small ears alertly pointed forward to discover the source of the danger. The mysterious lady rose also and turned around. Her crystal voice broke the silence of the surrounding forest, but not the mystic mood. As her green eyes met Merlyn's, a smile played at the corners of her ruby lips.

"Merlyn," she said.

"Nimue. May I introduce you to the Lady Guinevere?"

Nimue bowed slightly, wiping the smile from her lips. "Lady Guinevere, I humbly beg your pardon. It was not my intention to stray into your father's forest without permission. However, I needed to find this unicorn. It is very important. I hope you will understand."

Not used to being addressed with such authority, Guinevere became uncharacteristically tongue-tied, but only for a moment.

"I'm sure my father will have no problem with you being in the forest, particularly since you appear to be a friend of Merlyn's. My father thinks very highly of him," Guinevere replied, her eyes moving back and forth between Nimue and the unicorn.

"Thank you, Lady Guinevere."

"However, there is something that you could do for me," Guinevere said, unaware of the concerned look Merlyn was giving her.

"If it is in my power, then I will accommodate you, Lady Guinevere," Nimue replied.

"Would you let me pet the unicorn?" Guinevere asked, her

voice trembling with excitement.

Merlyn, having kept silent, now chuckled. Nimue glanced at him, and he nodded.

"It would be my pleasure, Lady Guinevere." Nimue motioned for Guinevere to move up beside her and nodded at the unicorn. It also moved closer to Nimue. "I'm afraid for all their majesty, they are just like any other horse. They like to be scratched around their ears," she said, smiling.

Slowly, so as not to frighten the unicorn, Guinevere held out her hand for it to smell. The warm, moist breath caressed her palm and sent shivers down her back. Without realizing it, Guinevere held her breath as she gently ran her hand tentatively over the soft nose. Then, breathing slowly, she reached up with her hand to the unicorn's ears. Wisps of the cloud-white mane shifted across her hand like silk. She scratched the unicorn's ears and was rewarded with a soft nicker as the unicorn gently nudged Guinevere in the chest.

With sparkling eyes and a grin that just grew wider, Guinevere smiled back at Nimue and Merlyn.

"I have never touched anything so magnificent before!" she exclaimed. "Why is it that I have never seen this unicorn? Cedwyn and I are around this forest all the time. Cedwyn!" Guinevere gasped. "Oh, how could I forget? He'll never forgive me. May I please go and get him?" She looked at Merlyn.

"I'm afraid not, Lady Guinevere," he replied, watching her smile fade. "The unicorn will not be here that long. Isn't that right, Nimue?"

Nimue nodded. "Merlyn is right, Lady Guinevere. I have come to take this one away. It is needed elsewhere."

"But it won't take long. Please!"

"Not this time, Lady Guinevere," Merlyn said.

"But why not? I don't understand."

Nimue looked at Merlyn. He put his arm around Guinevere's shoulders. "For many centuries," he began, "the unicorns have been hunted by all kinds of people. They considered it quite a feat to track one down and kill it."

"No!"

"Yes. You see, the unicorn is not just an ordinary animal. It's also magical, and with that magic comes power," Merlyn continued. "And man has always wanted to be more powerful."

"And so, Lady Guinevere," Nimue broke in, "unicorns have become very rare and show themselves to humans only when there is no choice. When the time comes, unicorns pick the person who will take their life and respect them in their death."

"You mean this unicorn has come here to die?" Guinevere cried. "But why? No one will harm it in this forest! My father will make sure of that."

"My Lady, this one has not come just to die," Nimue continued. "Unicorns have magical powers that are needed for people to live. They carry in their blood antidotes to poisons that otherwise would kill many people."

"But that's not the unicorns' fault! They don't deserve to die just so that we may live," Guinevere protested.

"There you are wrong," Merlyn said. "Unicorns know why they are on this earth and have no concerns about leaving it in the correct way. Long before man populated the world as he does now, unicorns were given life and the ability to sustain human life. They understood that then and understand that now."

"But..."

"Look at this one. Does it look sad, afraid?" Merlyn asked.

Guinevere looked carefully at the unicorn eating out of Nimue's hand. It was calm and totally unafraid. Guinevere looked back at Merlyn. "No."

"All creatures know that their time in this world is limited. And they also understand that they have a purpose that must be fulfilled before they leave. This unicorn knows that and comes willingly to Nimue who reveres and respects it. The blood will be treasured and used only when it is of the utmost importance. But, in order for that to happen, Nimue and others like her must already have the antidotes in hand when the time comes. Otherwise, they will fail in their attempt to save human lives," Merlyn finished.

"Does it hurt?" Guinevere asked, her brown eyes glistening with unshed tears.

"No, I use the magic given to me to lead the unicorn to a dignified and gentle end," Nimue replied.

"Unicorns have long and full lives," Merlyn added. "This one is over two hundred years old. They are not afraid when the time comes for this life to end. In fact, they eagerly look forward to their next life."

"They live again? How is that possible?"

"All things are possible in a world filled with magic. Look around you, Lady Guinevere," Merlyn said. "See all the magic that you live with every day? Trees sprout up without anyone planting them. Animals of all kinds continue to breed in spite of being hunted endlessly. Why, the birth of human babies is magical in its process. And further proof of that magic is standing right in front of you," Merlyn explained. "Do not despair. Everyone and everything is here for a purpose. All we have to do is make sure that we fulfill that purpose. And this unicorn will do that tonight by going with Nimue."

Guinevere gazed once more upon the pure and innocent unicorn. Her heart ached at the thought of such a creature dying. The moonlight shining down cast a ghostly haze over the unicorn, illuminating it. At the same time, its outline began to fade, almost as if the unicorn were not all there.

"Merlyn, why does the unicorn look so different?"

"Because it and Nimue are already on their way."

"But the unicorn still doesn't show any fear. It looks as it did when I scratched its ears," Guinevere said, not understanding the significance of what was happening.

"That's because there is nothing to fear. Nimue is taking care of it. That's why it chose Nimue," Merlyn explained.

"I hope that I find someone like Nimue to take care of me."

"I hope so too," Merlyn replied. "But look, they are almost gone."

Guinevere turned and saw that the outline of the unicorn and Nimue was fading into nothing. The moonlight dimmed and faint outlines of leafy branches could be seen where Nimue and the unicorn once stood.

Tears were trickling down Guinevere's cheeks. Wiping them away with her hand, she turned back to Merlyn.

"I want to live my life like the unicorn, graceful and regal. I want to live my life doing what I was put on this earth for and do it well. I want to be able to go to that magical world where Nimue is taking the unicorn," Guinevere said between sniffles. "Do you think that I will be able to do that?"

"Lady Guinevere, your path in life, like that of the unicorn, will not be smooth. At times it will even be hard. When those times come, remember what you witnessed here tonight, and that may help you," he said. "But, even unicorns sometimes trust the wrong people, the wrong feelings, or stray from their selected path. And if that happens to you, you must have the courage and the strength to find your way back again."

"Do you mean that my life might not end as the unicorn's?" Guinevere asked.

"That remains to be seen. Sometimes our paths are harder than they should be. And sometimes, the magic just isn't strong enough."

"Do you know your path?"

"Yes, I do. But it is not for me to reveal to anyone," Merlyn said.

"Do you know my path?"

"Some, Lady Guinevere, some."

"Can you tell me?"

"That would be abusing my magical powers. But tomorrow I can tell you a little of what awaits you."

"Tomorrow?"

"Tomorrow," Merlyn repeated. "For now, we had best get back before we are discovered. Even magicians like myself can be in trouble with the king."

Guinevere smiled, wiping the last of her tears away.

"Can I at least tell Cedwyn about the unicorn? He'll feel so bad that he wasn't able to be here."

"No, you cannot tell anyone, not even Cedwyn. Word cannot get out about a unicorn being here. Hundreds of people would swarm into the forest, and those who didn't would be certain you had lost your mind to even think unicorns were real. Promise that you will tell no one."

She hesitated. "I promise. No one will know that a unicorn was in the forest tonight," she said. "Will you see Nimue again?"

"Yes," he replied, the word hanging heavy in the night.

"Will you ask her if the unicorn made it safely to the other world?"

"Yes, I will. But now we need to get back."

Guinevere nodded, took one last glance where Nimue and the unicorn had stood, and obediently followed Merlyn.

Merlyn said nothing further until they reached the outer door. There he stopped. She looked up at him expectantly.

"Lady Guinevere," he said. "You must cease roaming about at night on your own and pay more attention to where you go during the day. The time is at an end when you can roam about at will."

"What do you mean?"

"Just what I said. With your thirteenth Birth Day the day after tomorrow, you will not be a little girl anymore. Your people have tolerated your childish ways and laughed at your amusing antics. But, upon your thirteenth Birth Day, they expect you to cease your adventurous ways and take your role as Lady of the Castle seriously. You will have great responsibilities, and your people need to know and see that you are able to carry out your duties."

"But, I like being a princess. How can my people--Who are my people?" she questioned in midstream.

"Your people are your father's people. They will transfer their complete loyalty over to you upon his death or when he defers to you and your husband."

"Well, Father is not ready to die, and I'm certainly not planning on marrying any time soon. So, why can't I just keep on the way I have been? I like being a child," she replied, stamping her foot and forgetting her earlier pledge to be like the unicorn.

"Because, like the unicorn, you must accept what your role is and will be. It may not always be to your liking. However, as a princess, you will do as you are expected. And part of that is growing up, whether you want to or not. No one ever truly knows what the future may hold, and we must be ready for whatever comes our way."

"Well, I don't think it's fair."

"Not much is fair when you have responsibilities," Merlyn added, his thoughts returning to his own future. "Now, get up to your room and hope that no one saw you leave. And no more wandering about at night for any reason, understand?"

"Yes, Merlyn," Guinevere replied with a sadness in her voice.

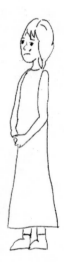

CHAPTER 5

BETRAYAL

The castle had been alive with activity for a couple of hours when Brynwyn climbed the stairs to Guinevere's room. She knocked on the wooden door.

"Lady Guinevere, are you awake?" Brynwyn's voice filtered through the sleep surrounding Guinevere. "Lady Guinevere?"

"Yes, I'm awake." Guinevere struggled to rise. "How early is it?"

"Time for you to be up and about. Lessons need to be done, and your father wants to see you."

"Why doesn't he just come up here?"

"Because he's the king, and you have to obey when he summons you, even if you are the princess," Brynwyn replied.

"All right," Guinevere mumbled back. "What good is it being a princess if I can't even sleep in?"

"Try going to bed when you're sent instead of sneaking out at night, and you won't have any trouble getting up in the morning," came Brynwyn's reply as her footsteps receded on the stone floor.

"Oh no," Guinevere muttered, storming around her room looking for clothes to put on. "If Brynwyn knows, then Father probably does too." She paused as she pulled a fresh tunic over her head. She continued her tirade as she brushed out her hair and tied it back with a leather strap. "I'm probably going to be forbidden outside the castle walls. Some way to treat a princess." She continued grumbling as she made her way to the throne room.

She hesitated at the door, not wanting to enter. This was not one of her favorite spots in the castle, even though her father spent most of his time here. The vastness of it made her feel uncomfortable. This was where her father conducted business, and it was stark and empty of welcoming items. The emblem of her father's kingdom, the upright bear holding a snake in its mouth, dominated the wall behind his long desk and overshadowed the two chairs situated in front. The bear was not meant for children. Off to the right an entryway led to the great gathering room. Inside that room stood the huge round table made for her grandfather during his days on the throne.

With her hands folded in front of her, Guinevere waited for her father to take notice and beckon her into the room. Possibly this was why she disliked this place so much. For as long as she could remember, she was trained to wait until called before entering.

She remembered once running in to tell her father of a secret place she and Cedwyn had found in the stable. While he had listened to her, Guinevere sensed that she had done something wrong. Only when she finished telling her story did she realize that someone else was in the room. Her father nodded and then quietly but sternly told her that any further conversation would have to wait until supper. Never again had she entered the throne room without permission.

King Leodegrance glanced up from his ledger and smiled as he greeted his daughter.

"Good morning, Guinevere. Come in and give your father a hug."

She did so, unsure yet if she was in trouble. Her father's arms felt strong around her small body, and Guinevere relaxed, feeling secure and sure of her father's love.

"Did you enjoy the feast last night?"

"Oh, yes! The wonderful food and the bard! Cedwyn never tired of watching all the knights. He wants to be one some day, you know."

"Yes, he has told me many times, but he still has a few years yet." King Leodegrance paused. "What did you think of King Arthur?"

"He was all right. I liked his dragon banner. Dragons are such fascinating creatures. I only wish I could see one," Guinevere added.

"That is not possible because dragons are mythical creatures."

"But so are unicorns, and I saw one of those!" She clasped her hand over her mouth, remembering Merlyn's warning not to tell anyone.

Her father's dark eyes bored into her. "What do you mean you saw a unicorn?" he asked.

"Ahem," came a voice from behind her, interrupting the king.

Guinevere turned, her eyes on Merlyn as he came into the room. He shook his head ever so slightly, but she knew what he meant.

"Sorry to be late, Your Highness."

"What? Oh, that's all right. You have missed nothing," the king replied.

"Well, let's get on with it, shall we?" Merlyn said.

She looked from one to the other curiously.

"Guinevere," her father continued, "we were talking about King Arthur."

As he paused, she nodded, unsure of what was coming.

"Let me go over a little background for you," her father said. "You may not be aware of it, but King Arthur is poised to be the next king of this entire country, from the North Sea to the big ocean. Land, Guinevere, that even I have not seen. It is his plan to bring together all of the kings under one banner, the dragon, just like his father, King Uther Pendragon, did. Except that King Arthur plans to bring them in peacefully and unite them to protect the entire nation instead of just their own kingdoms.

"Also, unlike his father, his chief concern then will be the welfare of all the people. He is hoping to find a national unity that will allow the country to prosper peacefully and still remain strong against its enemies. Quite a unique undertaking. Did I leave anything out, Merlyn?" King Leodegrance asked, pausing to allow Merlyn to add anything else.

"Nothing that I can think of. Any questions so far?"

"No, but this is interesting, and I guess because I am a princess," she paused and smiled at Merlyn to show him she remembered that part of their conversation late last night, "this is part of what I must learn if I am to be a good queen. Right?"

Her father glanced questioningly at Merlyn, who nodded and then replied, "Yes, Guinevere, that is right."

"Then I don't have any questions."

"Well then, to continue," her father said. "In order to unite the country under one banner, King Arthur is going to require assistance from all the kings. Assistance like knights willing to ride under his banner, while still retaining their allegiance to their king as well as to Arthur. A certain amount of food stores must be diverted to feed his growing army, and weapon and armor production will need to be increased across the kingdoms. Additionally, support staff from all the castles will be sent to maintain Arthur's troop movements across the country."

"And," Merlyn picked up, "Arthur's going to make his headquarters at the castle in Camelot. He has been living outside of there for several years now, and once the castle is restored, it will be big enough to support the extra troops and people. It will be fairly easy to defend because of its position atop a small hill. Also, the forest will be cleared all around the castle for quite some distance back to avoid having an enemy approach unseen."

"How far is Camelot from here?" Guinevere asked, looking from Merlyn to her father.

Merlyn answered her. "It's about a five day ride without any carts. To move people and supplies from here to Camelot would take about ten days."

"That sounds like a fun trip. Imagine the places you could explore along the way!" Guinevere added, somewhat excited. "I suppose that the feast last night was like saying yes to everything King Arthur wanted?"

"Yes, it was," her father answered, somewhat surprised at his daughter's grasp of the situation. "But there is also more." He glanced at Merlyn, who nodded.

"Guinevere, there is one more thing that King Arthur has requested."

She sat up a little straighter in her chair, concerned by the look on her father's face. She glanced at Merlyn, but he betrayed nothing. She turned her attention back to her father. Somehow she knew what came next concerned her and her future. She became nervous, not sure she really wanted to hear.

"Yes, Father?" she said, trying to sound confident, but failing.

"One thing that a king of Arthur's stature needs is someone by his side to assist him in spreading his ideas across the country and to help him in attaining his goal. This person needs to be strong-willed and someone that most of the people already know and respect, if only because of who that person is. There will be many opportunities to earn the people's true respect by Arthur's side." King Leodegrance paused, swallowing hard and somewhat hesitant to continue. A glance at Merlyn restored his confidence.

"What King Arthur asked last night, Guinevere, was for your hand in marriage as his Queen." His eyes locked with hers. "And I agreed."

Guinevere sat there, stunned. She looked at Merlyn and then back at her father. A couple of times she opened her mouth to reply but nothing came out. Neither man spoke, either out of fear or out of respect. They both knew Guinevere's independent streak and waited for the explosion that they knew might come.

"Marriage," she whispered, disbelief showing in her voice.

Both men nodded.

"But, I am only twelve..."

"Thirteen tomorrow," Merlyn interrupted.

"And it won't be for two more years, until you are fifteen," her father added. "A perfectly acceptable age for marriage. Your mother married me when she was fifteen."

"Arthur is a good person and will be a great king, Guinevere," Merlyn said. "I have watched and guided his growth from the time he was born."

"Guinevere," her father said, "as a princess, this is one of the expectations. You have known from the beginning that you would have certain responsibilities, including marriage when the time came and a kingdom to rule."

"But how could you do such a thing and not even talk to me about it?" Guinevere asked, regaining some of her thought process.

"But I *am* talking to you about it."

"After the decision has already been made!" Guinevere replied, her voice rising as the realization of the decision set in.

"Guinevere," Merlyn interrupted.

"And you. My friend! Did you know about this last night? In the hall? In the forest?" she asked, as she rose from her chair.

"Yes."

"Guinevere!" her father interjected.

"No! Arthur's too old! I don't like him! I don't want to be married!" Guinevere cried out, all of her doubts and fears about turning thirteen present in those words.

"He's only eight years older. You will have plenty of opportunities to learn to like him. And, princesses are supposed to be married!" Merlyn answered her, trying to keep the frustration out of his voice.

"I will not marry him, and you cannot make me!"

"You *will* marry him because not only am I your father, I am also the King, and my wishes will be obeyed. Now, sit down so that we may finish discussing this in a dignified manner," her father's stern voice commanded.

"No!"

"Guinevere!"

"No, no, no!" she repeated, her voice shaking as sobs overcame her, and her world crashed around her.

Merlyn put his hands on her shoulders and firmly sat her down.

Amid Guinevere's sniffles, the king further outlined what had been discussed. King Arthur would make frequent appearances at the castle--however, urgent business would prevent him from attending Guinevere's Birth Day tomorrow--so that he and

Guinevere could become acquainted. During the two years, there was no reason for the two of them not to become friends.

"After all Guinevere, your mother and I were the best of friends before we married. Our friendship served us well in our marriage and in ruling the kingdom," her father said in his most reassuring voice.

Guinevere sat, still sniffling, listening, but looking at the floor.

"Then," the king continued, "on your fifteenth Birth Day, you and King Arthur will be formally betrothed and a wedding date set for later that year. When you are settled in Camelot, then I will send your grandfather's round table to both of you as a wedding present."

Guinevere's head popped up.

"Grandfather's round table?! You promised him Grandfather's round table knowing that Grandfather gave it to *me*?" Guinevere asked with disbelief, rising once more out of her chair. The full realization that her life was no longer to be her own became abruptly clear.

"Now, Guinevere..."

"No! No! I will not have my grandfather's gift given away. No! And furthermore, I am not going to marry King Arthur, or anyone for that matter. And you can't make me. You can't make me!" Guinevere ran out of the throne room, crying.

King Leodegrance started after her, but Merlyn stopped him.

"Give her time to calm down. She has to come to terms with quite a bit. And although we both know that she has your temper, she also has Lady Roslyn's ability to reason out what is best. We just need to give her time," Merlyn advised.

King Leodegrance sat back down and sighed.

"Merlyn, it is times like these that I wish Roslyn was still here. She always understood what Guinevere was thinking or going through. Me, what I know best is how to command an army and run a kingdom, not how to raise a princess," the king said wearily.

"You have raised her just fine. In fact, she is becoming more and more like you every day: strong-minded and compassionate."

"I wonder if that is for the good."

"Only time will tell. Only time will tell."

"Yes, it will. But I am glad that business will keep Arthur away tomorrow. I do not think that he would particularly like this Guinevere."

"I think Arthur would see that as part of her attraction."

"I hope you are right," the king replied, shaking his head.

CHAPTER 6
RUNAWAY

Guinevere ran out the door of the keep, shading her eyes against the bright sun. Between her tears and the sunlight she was unable to see clearly. Suddenly she found herself falling toward the ground.

"Ouch!" a small voice cried. "Guin'ver, look out!"

Landing in a heap on the dusty ground, Guinevere sat up and brushed herself off. Cedwyn also brushed the dirt off his face and out of his hair. Slowly standing up, Guinevere continued to clean off her tunic.

"Sorry."

"What's the matter?"

"Fathers can be so mean some times!"

"I know. My mum's always saying if Father were home, then I'd be sure to get a lickin' every day. But she doesn't have the time," Cedwyn replied.

Guinevere managed a small smile. "Thanks for trying to make me feel better."

"So, what's the matter? What did your father do?"

"Just because he's King, he thinks he can make decisions for me without even con...consulting me. It just isn't right! I'm not going to stay here and do something that I don't want to do."

"So, what are you going to do?" Cedwyn asked, getting up and brushing off the seat of his trousers.

"I...I...I'm going to run away. That's what I'm going to do. And right now!" Guinevere stomped off to the side entrance she had used last night.

"I'm comin' too," Cedwyn said.

"I don't know. Your mom might worry about you."

"Naw, she won't. At least not any more than your father," he said, looking up at Guinevere. "Anyway, she'll be all right as long as I'm home before dark."

Guinevere glanced at Cedwyn strangely, shook her head, and went out the gate. If she had looked up, she would have seen two figures watching her from a high window, concern showing on both of their faces.

Once out of the castle, Guinevere skirted the forest and headed toward the vast plain laying between the main road and the forest.

"Where we gonna run to?" Cedwyn asked.

"The hunters come from beyond that plain. There must be a road there that people do not use all the time. I'll bet there's even a stream and food and wood to build a shelter," she replied, excitement at her forthcoming independence creeping into her voice. She would be in charge of her life. Her footsteps quickened at the prospect.

"What kind of food? You mean like veg'ables?"

"Sure, I bet there's lots of vegetables. And also rabbits. We'll be able to catch a rabbit and eat it!"

"A rabbit?! Com' on. I want to have something other than rabbits. We always get in trouble when we mess with rabbits."

"Oh, all right. We'll just have vegetables and mayhap some quail or some other animal."

"That sounds good. How long till we get to the stream?"

"I'm sure it's just up over that rise. We should be there before long."

Guinevere picked up the pace a bit, anxious to find the stream and know that she had successfully run away. Cedwyn kept pace with her for quite a while, but climbing up the hill, his short legs tired, unable to keep up with her long ones.

"Guin'ver? Can't we slow down?" Cedwyn asked, making his way around a patch of scrub brush.

"Not yet. We need to get to the top of this rise to see the stream on the other side."

"But my legs are tired. We must of been climbin' for hours." Then he turned and looked behind to see how far they had come. "Guin'ver!"

"Oh, all right. I'll slow down."

"Guin'ver! I can't see the castle! Are we lost?" he asked, his voice breaking slightly in fear.

Guinevere also looked, trying to keep calm when she couldn't see the castle. Then, far off to the left, just a tiny speck in the distance, there it was. She breathed, not realizing she had been holding her breath.

"There. To the left, just beyond the edge of the trees. See the castle? It almost looks like a dot," she said, pointing and turning Cedwyn's head in the right direction.

"I think I see it. Yes, I see it!" he answered with relief. "Are we going to rest now?"

"Just a short one. We're going to get hungry and thirsty soon, so we need to find the stream and some vegetables." Sitting down on the lush grass, she stared at the dot in the distance that was her home.

Hard to believe that last night she had been so happy. Now, her world had fallen apart. *It's not that I don't expect to get married. I know I must. But not now, not so soon.* And to spring it on her and not give her the opportunity to participate in the decision stung like the bee that had bitten her last summer. Suddenly, the magic of the unicorn seemed so far away. Her eyes started to water. She blinked and tried to wipe the tears away before Cedwyn saw them, but she couldn't.

"What's the matter? Why are you crying again? Is it because of that decision your father made?"

Guinevere nodded in reply.

"What do you have to do? Is that what the king and Merlyn

were talkin' about last night in the hall after everyone left?"

"It must be," she said, wondering if Merlyn had known even in the forest. "When did you see them?"

"I sneaked back into the hall after everyone had gone to bed to see if there was any more circlette left. I saw them with their heads together, but they didn't see me. They were discussin' some secret."

Shaking her head, Guinevere said, "That's why Father waited for Merlyn before he said anything to me. They came up with this idea between themselves." She felt so betrayed.

"So, what is it that you have to do? Why have we run away from home?"

"My Father the King and apparently Merlyn have decided that I am to marry King Arthur in two years and become his Queen. I'll have to leave the castle, my home, you, and everything I've grown up with," she added, not realizing that Cedwyn was staring at her with his mouth wide open.

"He even promised Grandfather's round table to King Arthur. All without asking!" She finished, sure that she had stated her point clearly. Her eyes strayed to the hand that Arthur had kissed. Quickly she averted them.

"Are you sure they said King Arthur?" Cedwyn asked, his amazement showing in his voice.

"Oh yes! I'm sure."

"That's fantastic! He's gonna be a great king! He's gonna bring all of England together. I heard some of the knights talking about him last night. They said that he is the bravest and best warrior they have ever seen. And the smartest!" He looked at Guinevere and shook his head. "And you are gonna be his Queen!" Disbelief washed over him. "I wish someone would make a decision like that for me!"

"Really? Then you can marry King Arthur!" she said, standing up and stamping her foot. Then she turned and stomped up the rise.

"Wait! Guin'ver!"

She ignored him as she crested the top of the rise and disappeared from view. Abruptly she stopped, Merlyn's betrayal on her mind. *That's what it was, betrayal. Telling me that story about the unicorn just to get me to think that I should be like that.* She kicked a rock across the path. *I won't marry someone I don't know just to help out the country!* Then she remembered Arthur's smile as she had left the feast. She didn't know what to think or do. Her simple life had become very confusing.

She continued down the hill lost in thought. Not watching where she was walking, she found herself in a grove of willows. Hearing the splashing of the water she followed the sound to its banks and sat down, her knees pulled up to her chin. This was where Cedwyn found her a short time later.

"Did you find any veg'ables?" he asked, slightly out of breath.

Silently, she picked up something green and handed it to him. He looked at it, tried it, and then spit it out.

"Uck! That tastes just like a weed!"

"Well, what did you expect?" Her voice was still angry. "Carrots, lettuce, and asparagus like home?"

He nodded, confusion etched on his face at her tone.

"Well, this is what wild vegetables look and taste like."

"In that case, I don't think I'm very hungry. Does the water taste different 'cause it's wild?" he asked, his childish innocence lost on her.

Her answer was a sharp glare. Silently he stooped beside the stream and cupped his hands. Dipping into the cool water, he smiled as he tasted it.

"Hey. This tastes just like our water!"

"Sometimes I wonder where your brain is."

"It's right here, in my head, where it's 'posed to be."

"Oh forget it. I've got to figure out what to do," she said, leaning her chin on her hand.

"I know what you do," Cedwyn said quietly.

She looked at him.

"You marry King Arthur and become Queen Guinevere." He grinned. "Then you make me a squire. You have to be a squire, you know, before you can be a knight," Cedwyn stated. "Then when I'm ready, King Arthur will be able to make me a knight."

"So, you think I should marry King Arthur. And what if I decide that I do not *want* to marry him? What then?"

"But how can you do that?"

"I don't know, but I bet I can," she said, although Merlyn's words about being unable to pick her future kept poking into her thoughts. Also, the vision of the unicorn fading away with Nimue kept pushing its way into her mind along with Arthur's smile.

"My mum tells me that children must always obey their parents 'cause they are older and know better," he said.

"But I don't know Arthur. I don't even know if I would like being a queen."

"But don't you like being a princess?"

She nodded.

"Then, you should like being a queen."

"I don't know. I still think that I should have some say in what concerns me," she said, determined to protest, although Arthur had seemed nice.

"But you will."

"How do you know?"

"Because in all the stories my mum tells me, the king picks the men from the princess' people to go with them and become loyal knights. That means that you could have King Arthur pick me." He looked at her with pleading eyes. "I've always wanted to be a knight. I would be a good knight, Guin'ver. You know that. Look at all the adventures we have gone on and the hunting trips and... and this one. This run-away. This is a long way from the castle, and I'm not even afraid, much," Cedwyn finished.

Guinevere broke out in laughter.

"You could be right," she conceded, thinking that if what he said was true, then being like the unicorn might not be so bad. "But even if I don't like being a queen much, it will be nice to have you there so we can have more adventures."

"Do you really mean it?"

"Yes," she said, smiling. "Yes."

"Let's go back to the castle so I can tell my mum. Will she be surprised! I'm gonna be a squire!" Cedwyn started up the rise and then stopped. "Guin'ver, are we done runnin' away?"

"We're done running away. Let's go home," she said, though still unsure of her future.

"I bet we could get some real veg'ables!"

It sure is taking a lot longer to go home than it took to run away, she thought as she watched the sun sink toward the horizon. Picking up her pace, she motioned for Cedwyn to do the same. Hungry, he offered no complaints.

Finally, the main castle gate came into view. It was close enough to supper that the surrounding plain was deserted. Only the guards on the parapets were visible. However, upon closer inspection, Guinevere spotted a figure waiting just outside the gate.

"That sure looks like my mum. Are we goin' to have to do extra chores again like yesterday? I just wanna eat supper. I don't wanna be in trouble."

"Don't worry. I think your mum is waiting to talk to me."

"Oh good," Cedwyn said, relieved. Guinevere just glanced at him.

"Good evening, My Lady. Cedwyn, your supper is on the table. Best get cleaned up and eat," Brynwyn said, giving him a push toward the gate.

"I will, but Mum, Guin'ver's gonna let me be her squire so I can be a knight!"

"That's wonderful, Cedwyn. Now, though, future knights need to eat a good supper so they grow up strong."

"I know. Wait till I tell you about wild veg'ables and wild water!" he said as he made his way through the gate.

Guinevere stood there and waited for what she knew was coming. Since her mum's death, Brynwyn was always her father's choice for a woman to talk to Guinevere about things that needed attention.

"Lady Guinevere, I sincerely hope that you're not filling my son's head full of nonsense with this business about squires and knights. He looks up to you, he does," Brynwyn said, her brown eyes staring hard at Guinevere.

"No, Brynwyn. I would not hurt him for the world. I meant what I said. Cedwyn said that is how it is done in the stories that you tell him."

"Yes, the princesses in those stories do as their fathers ask and marry kings. They have to be queens to appoint squires. And even more importantly, they have to want to help their people and do what is best for them."

"I know. Cedwyn and I talked about it. I shouldn't have gotten mad at my father and Merlyn. I am a princess, and I know that one day I'll have to be a queen. I just wish it wasn't so soon. I like being a princess," she confessed, hanging her head down.

"I know you do, Lady Guinevere." Brynwyn gently lifted Guinevere's head. "But like your mum, you'll also make a great queen."

"I hope so," Guinevere replied, her brown eyes wet with unshed tears. "I guess I'd better find Father and tell him I'm sorry. Is he very mad at me?"

"One thing you will learn, Lady Guinevere. Fathers cannot stay mad at their daughters for long. That's the rule," Brynwyn said, giving Guinevere a gentle push. "So hurry up and see your father. Both you and Cedwyn have a big day tomorrow. It's your thirteenth Birth Day!"

Guinevere stood silently outside the throne room gathering her nerve. She knew her father would be angry with her outburst, especially since it happened in front of Merlyn. Taking a big breath, she crossed the threshold.

Her father glanced up from reading a parchment and looked down again.

Guinevere swallowed and just stood there. It was hard not to turn and run back out the way she had come. Still silent, she bowed her head and tried to keep the tears from flowing.

"Yes, Guinevere?" Her father's voice sounded more weary than angry. Glancing up, she saw his hand run through his hair and was surprised to see so much grey mixed with the black. She was used to the grey in his beard, that had always been there. She realized that her father was getting old.

"Father," she whispered, "I am sorry for my behavior earlier. I know better, but my temper just got in the way. I know that you and Merlyn are only doing what must be done." She stopped and hesitated, swallowed hard again and continued, feeling her father's dark eyes on her face. "I just wanted to be a princess for a while longer. I like being a princess. I understand now that I will like being a queen when it is time."

King Leodegrance looked sharply at his young daughter. "And how did you decide that?"

"Cedwyn told me. He said that if I enjoyed being a princess, I would enjoy being a queen also. And he is right," she added. "He also would not want to be my friend for long if I was the reason he could not become a squire."

"A squire?" She nodded. "I guess I will have to say something to Arthur about that," he added, smiling as he walked over to Guinevere.

Framing her small face in his strong hands, King Leodegrance looked into her eyes.

"Guinevere, you must understand that I would never let anything happen to you that I thought would cause you pain or not be good for you. I promised your mother that before she left us." He paused before continuing, his eyes roaming over her face. "You really are a lot like her, you know?"

Guinevere nodded. This was not the first time her father or others had mentioned the resemblance.

"However, you were also cursed with my temper, which Merlyn reminded me of this morning. So, while I was a bit angry earlier today, now I am just happy that your mother's temperament allowed you to understand what I did."

"I know that, Father. And I will be a good queen." She paused. "It was a surprise and a shock. It seems like children should get to be children longer."

"I suppose it does. But I am not getting younger, Guinevere. And I must know that you are cared for when it is time for me to join your mother."

The tears that Guinevere had held in so long now ran freely down her cheeks as she reached out and hugged her father.

King Leodegrance held her tight and fought back tears of his own.

"Don't worry, Guinevere. I have many years left yet. Enough

to see you married, and," he drew back from her, gently wiped her tears away, and smiled, "I plan to be able to play with my grand-children." He kissed her on the forehead and gently pushed her to-ward the door. "Now, go and get to bed. You want to be up early tomorrow for your thirteenth Birth Day!"

She smiled at him. "Good night, Father."

"Good night, Guinevere."

CHAPTER 7
THE BIRTH DAY

"No, put our tent over there by the main gate. That way people can buy a drink as soon as they come past the moat." The woman's voice drifted up through Guinevere's window.

She stirred and rolled over, pulling the quilt over her head. *Did I really agree to marry Arthur last night?* Doubt fell over her at the thought. She buried her head deeper under the quilt.

"You there. Help me take these horses over to the field by the paddock. The races won't be run 'til later. They don't need to be inside," said a man, his deep voice carrying up to Guinevere's room.

"Guin'ver! Guin'ver! Aren't you up yet?" This time it was Cedwyn's voice she heard. "Com'on Guin'ver. It's your Birth Day! People have been up and coming since before sunrise."

Guinevere sat up in bed. "At least Cedwyn will be happy that I'm marrying King Arthur, even if I'm not," she said aloud. She walked over and stuck her head out the window. There, two stories below, stood Cedwyn. Behind him, people, animals, and brightly colored tents filled the bailey courtyard. Just over the wall,

Guinevere could see the tops of more tents outside. People and animals were still traveling down the road to the castle.

"I'll be right down," she hollered.

"Hurry! Cook made fresh berry rolls and apple cider. I've already had some, but he said that I couldn't have any more till you came down to eat. So, hurry up!"

"I'm coming!" She got dressed in a pale yellow tunic, tied her hair back, and pulled on her soft leather shoes.

Cedwyn met her as soon as she came into the yard.

"How could you sleep so long? It's your Birth Day! I've been up for hours."

"I know. I'm sorry. You could have called me sooner."

"I would of, but my mum wouldn't let me. She said you were mentally tired, whatever that means, and that I had to wait. But I couldn't wait any longer. Com'on, Cook's set up outside the kitchen. Wait till you taste the berry rolls!" He ran ahead.

She followed, still troubled about her decision, but not for long. She was stopped several times on her way by well-wishers.

"Happy Birth Day, Lady Guinevere," an old gentleman from the stable said, as he led three horses out of the area. He bowed, and Guinevere nodded and thanked him.

"Lady Guinevere, Happy Birth Day," Maggie said, her arms full of fresh carrots.

"Thank you, Maggie."

Several other people also greeted Guinevere delaying her further. Seeing Cedwyn waiting up ahead, she smiled at him and tried to hurry.

Cook greeted them at the long table where he was busy getting food ready for the feast.

"Happy Birth Day, Lady Guinevere," he said, bowing.

"Thank you, Cook."

"I have some fresh warm berry rolls right here just for you," he said. Then glancing at Cedwyn with a slight frown, he added, "Your friend there would have been more than eager to down these along with the other six he has already eaten!"

Guinevere turned to Cedwyn, feigning surprise at his appetite.

"I told you I have been up for hours! I got hungry," he said defending himself. "And besides, you know that no one makes better berry rolls than Cook."

She laughed at that, her doubt about her decision receding behind her growing excitement. After all, it was her Birth Day. She took three of the warm rolls and let Cedwyn have the other three. Then filling cups with cider, they sat down to eat and watch the activity.

Guinevere bit into the warm roll and sighed, catching the fresh red berry filling with her tongue and finger as it dripped out of the roll.

"Told you they were good," Cedwyn said, a grin on his face and red berry filling running down his chin. A quick finger and tongue stopped the runaway berry.

From their position, they could see everything. Just inside the main gate, several brightly colored tents were pitched. A couple of groups had casks of ale and what looked like hard bread sitting on hides on the ground. At another tent, a lady was busy stringing up bracelets and necklaces of beads. Obviously she had come with the intention of selling or trading her beads as well as having a good time.

The sound of bells drew Guinevere's attention away from the gate. Under a bright green tent, a girl younger than she, dressed in a brown tunic and barefoot, helped an older heavyset woman string up jewelry. Around the girl's ankles bracelets of tiny silver bells jingled every time she moved.

"That's what I want to get today. I love the sound of those tiny bells," she said.

Cedwyn turned to look but wasn't impressed. His eyes were on another item.

"There," he said pointing to a black tent that was open on all sides. Underneath it was a small man covered in leather. In the center of the tent was an anvil and a fire pit. The man was bending over the anvil hammering a piece of metal. Satisfied, he stopped and held up a small dagger, still gleaming red from the heat. As they watched, he thrust the dagger down into a barrel of water. Steam rose from the water like the mist in the summer heat as the dagger was cooled. Then he placed it next to several others on a hide on the ground. The blacksmith Sauder stood watching and nodded his approval as he appraised the dagger.

"Think of the animals I could hunt with that!" Cedwyn said. His eyes sparkled with the thought of owning such a weapon. "We could even go after rabbits and cut wild veg'ables!"

"We could, but that must be awfully expensive," Guinevere replied.

"I know, but I've saved money from doing chores for other people, even your father."

"We'll go over later and see what it costs."

"I heard someone say something about a man who swallows swords and fire. He's supposed to be in a tent outside the wall. Do you want to go and see?" he asked.

"Yes. Mayhap the magicians are out there too," Guinevere said as she scrambled to her feet.

Outside the castle gate, they gasped at the sight that greeted them. A sea of multicolored tents filled up the meadow like buttercups did in the late spring. Threading their way among the tents, Guinevere and Cedwyn passed by a multitude of strangely dressed people and a pack of dogs in search of small creatures they could chase. Like the children, the dogs were enjoying the festive atmosphere. One group of men and women wore hides that were dyed various shades of yellow, black, and green. Another was dressed in animal fur, even in the late summer heat. Cedwyn wrinkled up his nose as they passed and walked a little faster.

Several tents sheltered a variety of foodstuffs: hard bread, fried bread dough coated with honey and cinnamon, different types of jerky, some porridges, and an abundance of fresh fruit and vegetables. They continued to weave in and around the numerous tents, always on the lookout for the fire eater and the magicians. Although full from a late breakfast, they sampled different foods as the morning wore on.

With the sun high in the blue and white speckled sky, the heat from the people and the dust kicked up by the livestock made them thirsty. There was no shortage of drinks, but over half were off limits to them. They gladly tasted the different cider flavors as they continued to wander.

When the trumpet sounded for the afternoon games, Guinevere and Cedwyn had yet to find the fire eater or the magicians. However, they were so full of food and drink that the games and the feast that evening were not even appealing.

"My stomach hurts," Cedwyn said.

"I know. Mine does too. Let's go back and just sit for a while."

"But that was the trumpet for the start of the games."

"If I try to play any games now, I will vomit!"

"Maybe Merlyn can give us something so we feel better."

By the time they found Merlyn, both were looking green. He chuckled and gave them a potion, but it took nearly an hour to work. During that time, they sat on the chairs and watched the other kids play Fox and Geese. By the time the fox had changed players four or five times, the game was halted. Everyone then lined up to pick sides for kickball. Feeling better, Guinevere and Cedwyn rushed over to join in. Because it was Guinevere's Birth Day, once she came onto the field, the others made her one of the leaders and let her have first pick. Naturally, she chose Cedwyn first.

Both sides lined up on the playing field. One person from each team guarded their goal on the opposite side. Each team provided two headers to retrieve the ball at the start of the game and after a score. They also watched for the opportunity to steal the ball from the other team. The remaining seven members tried to block the other team from reaching their end and also tried to move the ball to their goal. It made for riotous fun for players and spectators alike.

Merlyn volunteered to put the hide-covered ball into play. Using his magic, he elevated it and then let it drop. Both sides' headers scrambled for the ball. Guinevere's team just barely snatched it from the other team's headers. Then the chase started.

Players passed the ball around, moving toward their goal. A couple of times the other team stole it, but Guinevere's team got it back. Suddenly the ball neared their opponent's goal when the players defending moved the wrong way. The player nearest the ball gave it a firm kick, and it went in between the guard's legs. The spectators cheered. The kicker threw his arms up in the air in victory. It was Cedwyn!

The next round resulted in a score for the other side. After a se-
ries of plays in which the teams traded the lead, players and spectators alike were growing tired and thirsty. Guinevere's team
controlled the ball, but could not score. The growing number of
spectators alternately cheered and groaned.

Just when it seemed that another attempt to move the ball was
going to be thwarted, Cedwyn moved in to kick. His foot con-
nected to the ball, and it took off. He started to cheer, but his arms
fell to his side. He stood staring at where he had kicked the ball.
The other children also stopped and stood with their mouths gap-
ing.

Guinevere cheered as the ball passed over the heads of the
other team and over the head of the guard and down into the goal.
Merlyn stood smugly on the sidelines while King Leodegrance patted him on the back.

"Guinevere's team wins!" a voice yelled out. "Three cheers for
Lady Guinevere!"

Good-naturedly, the crowd cheered her, and the players all
came forward to offer their congratulations. Some grumbled about
wizards who did not know their place, but no one said it very loud
or really in anger. No one wanted a wizard mad at them.

The crowd dispersed, mostly to go and set up for the banquet
feast. Because of the number of people, it was to be held outside in
the courtyard. The tired players walked to the cider barrels for a
drink. They decided to play one last game of hide and seek before
supper. They enjoyed that game the most because the castle had
such wonderful places to hide. Inside half empty grain barrels was
the favorite. The older kids liked to hide along the parapet so that
they could jump down and scare the little ones.

When the horn sounded, children and adults made way for
King Leodegrance and Lady Guinevere to begin the feast. Once
they were seated and served, everyone else filled their plates. Soon
the only sounds heard in the bailey courtyard were the scraping of
forks and the clanging of tin cups full of ale and cider.

"Guinevere," her father said as he wiped his mouth and beard.

"Yes, Father?"

"Are you still feeling okay about becoming a queen?"

She hesitated, looked down at her plate and remembered the feel of Arthur's breath on her hand. She raised her eyes to meet her father's.

"Yes, I am, most of the time. I know that sometimes I will get scared, but I know that you, Merlyn, Cedwyn, and many others will be there for me. It will be all right." She smiled at her father with more confidence than she felt, but she was determined to follow the path of the unicorn. And Arthur could be called good looking when his smile softened the scar.

King Leodegrance returned his daughter's smile, silently thanking his wife Roslyn for passing her wisdom on to Guinevere.

As people finished eating, the noise in the courtyard grew. The king's men lit torches around the edges of the bailey. Smoke and burning oil mingled with the odors of dinner. People continued gossiping and trading news with their neighbors until everyone had eaten. Suddenly, a low sound echoed around the castle walls. Soon the entire crowd picked up the chant.

"Merlyn, Merlyn, Merlyn!"

Even King Leodegrance and Guinevere joined in. Merlyn could not refuse such a request. Graciously he stood up and walked toward the center of the courtyard as everyone moved to allow him room. Around the outside of the crowd, Cedwyn made his way to the vacant spot next to Guinevere.

"Are you really going to marry King Arthur?" he asked as he sat down.

"I guess so," she said. "I know I have to find the courage to honor my decision, but I'm scared."

"I'll be with you. I'll help you." He put his hand on her arm to show his support.

Grateful, she squeezed his small hand. "I know you will, and I'll need your help."

Merlyn held up his hands. The crowd quieted in anticipation. His magic and fireworks amazed everyone. Blazing colors of red, green, blue, and yellow lights crossed the courtyard and shot out from behind the parapets. Mystical creatures like unicorns and serpents suddenly appeared to inhabit many of the doorways leading into the bailey courtyard. Adults and children screamed with fear and laughter. But the best, Merlyn saved for last.

Suddenly high in the sky over the castle, a stream of fire burst forth! A tremendous roar followed that had all the children grabbing their parents' legs and hands. Unable to take their eyes from the sky, everyone watched in fascinated horror as a gigantic dragon circled the walls of the castle, fire alternating with roars coming out of its mouth. Several times it swooped down as if to devour the crowd in one gulp. During this whole time, Cedwyn clung to Guinevere, who held onto her father, her fingers gripping his arm and back.

Then the dragon flew high up in the sky and circled the castle a couple of times as if searching for prey. Its bright red eyes locked on Guinevere. She stared, unable to look away, her brown eyes wide open. The dragon turned and barreled down from the sky. Adults and children started to scream. Cedwyn tugged at Guinevere's hand to get her to run, but to no avail. She sat transfixed, unable to move.

The dragon came closer. The screaming grew louder. Cedwyn tugged harder.

Just as the dragon appeared to be reaching for Guinevere, it swept upwards with a roar. Red and yellow flames spewed out of its mouth. Then the flames turned to brilliant red, yellow, blue, and green flowers that floated down on Guinevere. The crowd erupted in cheers, laughter, and applause. Guinevere clapped her hands until they hurt while tears of relief and joy ran down her face. Cedwyn stood there, unable to comprehend what had just happened. When it made sense, he too started clapping wildly. Even King Leodegrance shouted with amazement.

As the crowd gradually broke apart for Merlyn, many proclaimed this a show to be remembered for a long time. When Merlyn finally made his way to King Leodegrance and Guinevere, they greeted him royally. The king hugged him and patted him on the back. Guinevere gave him a warm hug and kiss. Cedwyn just stood there, unsure of what to say. Merlyn patted his head.

"Oh, Merlyn," Guinevere said. "I don't know how to say thank you! I have never seen anything so wonderful."

"Neither have I," King Leodegrance added. "You have definitely outdone yourself tonight."

"Nothing should ever be ordinary for a princess destined to be the queen of all England," Merlyn replied. "We want everyone to remember her, and what better time to start than at her Birth Day celebration tonight? And what more fitting creature than the dragon that rides the standard of King Arthur?" Merlyn added, aware of Guinevere's sudden silence. "Besides," he said, looking specifically at Cedwyn, "I enjoy giving everyone a fright from time to time, right, Cedwyn?"

Cedwyn moved his mouth to answer, but all that came out was "Uh...yes!" The king laughed, as did the others. Then Merlyn took Guinevere and Cedwyn's hands.

"Now, though, a special treat just for the two of you." He paused, seeing Cedwyn's eager face and a bit of a sparkle coming back into Guinevere's eyes. "Tomorrow at the break of day, you both need to be up at sunrise and ready for a grand adventure. It seems that King Pellinore, his bratchet hound, and that darned Painted Dragon have gotten lost in the forest. I need some good hunters to help me find them, so off you both go to bed. I will see you first thing in the morning."

CHAPTER 8
FOREST MELEE

G uinevere stood by the door. In between glares at Cedwyn, she kept looking out into the bailey courtyard.

"Hurry up, Cedwyn. Merlyn's going to leave without us," she whispered, not wanting to wake Brynwyn.

"I'm comin'," he replied, pulling on his other shoe.

Ready at last, the two hurried toward the castle gate and Merlyn. The sun was just starting to peek over the horizon.

"Humph! About time!" Merlyn said as they reached him. "Not able to get enough sleep? Maybe dreaming of dragons?!" He chuckled as Cedwyn's expression betrayed the fact that he had had a very restless night. "Well, it's daylight now. Dragons sleep in the light so we should have a very uneventful trip. All we have to do is find King Pellinore and that darn bratchet dog! Let's hurry up now. We have plenty of forest to cover and who knows what we will come across," he finished as he marched out of the castle gate and toward the forest, his long strides threatening to leave them behind.

"Do dragons really sleep in the day? Merlyn, how come you said we would have an unev'ntful trip when we don't know what we will come across?"

Merlyn just chuckled and motioned them to follow. "One never knows what the forest will reveal, but at least it won't be dragons!"

"What does he mean, Guin'ver?" Cedwyn asked, confused by Merlyn's double talk.

"I'm not sure, but let's not let him get too far in front." She glanced ahead. Merlyn was just ducking under the edge of the forest canopy. Nervously, she looked around, mindful of the last time that she and Cedwyn had been in the forest. Thankfully, nothing appeared to be moving in the tall grass on either side of them.

"Do you think we'll run into that wild pig again? Will it remember that you were the one that shot it?" Cedwyn asked. He had additional questions, but Guinevere turned and put her finger to her lips.

"If you keep talking so loud, it *will* find us. So be quiet and hurry. Merlyn's already out of sight."

Cedwyn looked up the path, but Merlyn was nowhere to be seen. He started to panic. Once they stepped under the dark green forest canopy and out of the sunlight, Merlyn's flowing grey robe appeared just ahead of them. Cedwyn heard Guinevere's sigh echo his.

Merlyn waited until they caught up before choosing a hidden path through the scrub brush. The trio moved in deeper in the forest, Merlyn in the lead. Guinevere came next. She followed somewhat hesitantly, her and Cedwyn's run-in with the boar still vivid in her mind. Her heart raced faster at the thought of meeting another one.

Cedwyn came last, at times having to run to keep up with Merlyn's pace. Of course, it would have been easier if he hadn't kept stopping to investigate the brown and green vegetation all around. He wasn't looking for the bugs, worms, or small creatures common around the castle. No, what Cedwyn watched for was whatever Merlyn referred to when he told them that he didn't know what the forest had in store for them. He wanted to be ready, but for what he wasn't sure.

"Guin'ver?" he asked as he caught up to her where the path widened. "What do you think Merlyn thinks might be in the forest?"

"I don't know," she replied, catching herself looking around. "Let's just stay close. Merlyn can take care of anything that comes near."

"Now, I wouldn't be so quick to say that, Lady Guinevere," Merlyn said as he stopped. "Oh, the forest always has the typical inhabitants. Wild boar, deer, foxes, porcupines, rabbits, and an occasional leopard." They both shuddered at the mention of the leopard. "But remember," he continued, "forests have also been magical places for much longer than humans have been on this earth. Many creatures that man has never seen are still around, taking refuge deep in the forests where man seldom goes.

"Why, I have heard talk of people coming across a strange looking animal with the body of an eagle and the head of a leopard." Cedwyn looked at him with disbelief. "Now don't look like that, Cedwyn. We have no way of knowing if such an animal really exists unless we happen to cross its path. However, I myself have seen several animals that few even know exist. In fact," he said, putting his face down closer to Cedwyn's, "I have even seen unicorns!"

Guinevere gasped, her eyes meeting Merlyn's. At the slight shake of his head, she understood that she was still bound by her promise not to talk of her encounter with Nimue and the unicorn.

Cedwyn's blue eyes became enormous, but then narrowed as he tried to determine if Merlyn was really telling the truth.

"On my word of honor, Cedwyn. I have truly seen unicorns in the forests of England," Merlyn said solemnly. "And a more beautiful and majestic creature will never be found on earth again."

"For sure?"

"For sure."

"Wow, mayhap that's what's waiting for us." Cedwyn concluded.

"Mayhap. But if we spend much more time standing here, we will never find out. Off we go now." Merlyn turned and started off down the path with Guinevere and Cedwyn right on his heels.

Barely thirty minutes had gone by when he stopped and motioned them to do the same. He listened intently for a few moments, then turned to them.

"I think we may be in luck. Listen carefully. Hear the hurried approach of an animal?"

"What kind of animal?" Guinevere asked.

"And why is it hurr'ing?" Cedwyn asked.

Merlyn listened intently again.

"It appears to be a rabbit," he answered. "And it is hurrying because something is chasing it."

Just then, they all heard the faint but growing barking.

"It's the bratchet!" Cedwyn shouted. "Over here!" He ran into the scrub and grasses to the right.

"Wait for us!" Guinevere called as she bounded off after him.

"Wait for us," Merlyn grumbled as he followed her. "As if kids ever waited for anyone or anything!"

Guinevere and Merlyn hurried to catch up with Cedwyn, but branches that he had run under impeded their progress. Merlyn, in particular, found the cross country route difficult for a wizard of his height. Repeatedly branches grabbed at his flowing gown and tugged at his beard.

"You know," he shouted ahead as both children disappeared from view, "we could still catch the rabbit and the bratchet if we just followed the path a little farther!" Shaking his head, he continued ducking under branches while holding onto his hat.

Up ahead, the barking of the hound changed pitch. Instead of a lowing bark, the bratchet, catching sight of the rabbit, emitted a high shrill howl signaling the final capture.

At about the same time, Cedwyn also spotted the rabbit.

"There," he pointed to his left. "I'm going after the rabbit! Guinevere, catch the bratchet when he comes through the brush."

"Wait. We don't need the rabbit!"

"Yes we do!" he answered as he smiled. "That's our dinner!" Whooping like a madman, Cedwyn darted into the brush after the rabbit.

To her right, Guinevere heard the bratchet. Closer, its high-pitched howl hurt her ears. She positioned herself where she thought it would break through the brush.

Merlyn stopped as he caught up to Guinevere. She crouched on the ground, her arms open. Then the brush in front of her exploded.

Out came pieces of branches, leaves, and a brown blur. She appeared to hang onto the blur for a few seconds. Merlyn even heard her shout, "I've got you!" Then she flew backward, and the brown blur disappeared into the brush behind her, still howling.

Picking herself up before Merlyn could even react, Guinevere chased after the bratchet.

"Cedwyn," she shouted. "Look out! He got away! I'm coming!"

Cedwyn yelled back. "I've got the rabbit! I've got the rab...!"

Immediately, the forest erupted into children screaming and shouting, a rarely heard squeal from the rabbit, and the incessant howling of the bratchet. Merlyn was sure they were all being murdered and that he would have to answer to the king. He increased his speed and even jumped over small bushes in his hurry to reach them.

The scene that he came upon in the small clearing was beyond description, even for Merlyn.

Cedwyn, having caught the rabbit, held it by the ears, which the rabbit did not appreciate. Hence, the rabbit's squealing. The bratchet kept jumping up trying to latch onto the legs of the rabbit. Each time Cedwyn jumped up, the rabbit bounced out of the hound's reach. Hence, Cedwyn's screaming. Guinevere, hanging on to the bratchet, her fingers buried in brown fur, kept it from reaching the rabbit. Hence, the continued howling of the bratchet, and Guinevere's repeated warnings hollered at Cedwyn. Added to all this, arms, legs, tails, leaves, and dirt flew everywhere. Merlyn stood there stunned, unable to believe the sight before him.

"I say," Merlyn shouted. "Do you think we could calm down a bit?"

"Merlyn! Grab the bratchet! Help Guinevere," Cedwyn shouted while he continued to jump up, holding the rabbit just out of the bratchet's reach.

"No, Merlyn! I have him! Help Cedwyn!" Guinevere shouted, desperately hanging on to the brown fur as the bratchet struggled to be free.

Merlyn shook his white head and stared into the melee wondering if he could bring about some order. Deciding where to start was his first move. Assessing the situation, he settled on helping Guinevere hold the bratchet back. Both Cedwyn and the rabbit were evenly matched, but the training and instinct of the bratchet for its prey were showing their strain on Guinevere. Dirt and sweat covered her face and arms.

Her legs were so tangled up with the bratchet's that Merlyn had trouble telling hers from the hound's with all the dust swirling. Adding to the mess, the two continually rolled around on the ground further scattering leaves and kicking up more dirt. Guinevere's ragged breathing caused her to gasp for air as she desperately tried to hang on to the dog's neck.

The bratchet didn't weigh nearly as much as Guinevere, but its determination to reach the rabbit fueled its every movement. Virtually ignoring the weight around its neck, its deep-set eyes never left the rabbit in Cedwyn's hands. Every muscle in its body tensed each time the hound prepared to jump. Its short brown ears flickered only slightly each time one of the children hollered. And when the rabbit squealed, the hound's ears pointed straight at its prey.

Having chosen Guinevere as the object of his assistance, Merlyn advanced cautiously. He tried to dodge the legs and covered his mouth with his sleeve to avoid breathing in the dust. Several times he approached Guinevere, but each time jumped back as she and the bratchet bounced around. Realizing there was no way to help except by plunging into the fray, Merlyn sighed and dived in. No sooner had he secured his hold around Guinevere and the bratchet than things became worse than just the dust and hair in his mouth and eyes.

A piercing hunting horn sounded just beyond the clearing, adding another frantic sound to the battle. Merlyn tried to see who or what was coming without losing his hold on Guinevere and the bratchet. Through the flying dust, he just made out a black, green, and white blur coming out of the trees straight toward all of them. The horn blew again, but this time a man's shout followed.

"Onward brave hunter! Look out you miserable Painted Dragon! You will not get away this time! Onward!" King Pellinore's voice rang out loud.

"Oh no!" Merlyn hollered. "Pellinore, King Pellinore! You must turn away! Look out! Away! Aw....."

Merlyn felt the wind being knocked out of him as the Painted Dragon tromped on his chest in a valiant attempt to escape Pellinore. Knocked on his back, Merlyn only vaguely saw a black, green, and white shadow pass overhead. The screaming of the children increased. The struggle of the bratchet doubled. The Painted Dragon sailed overhead pursued by Pellinore. Unable to stop, Pellinore and his black charger bore down on the melee.

"Hit the dirt!" Merlyn tried to shout, short of wind and making a failed attempt to grab Guinevere and Cedwyn.

"Look out!" King Pellinore shouted. "I'm jumping!" With that he leaned low over the neck of the black charger, its front legs stretching up as its powerful back legs propelled Pellinore and horse up and over all.

Once clear, Pellinore blasted his horn again. The hound went crazy, broke Guinevere's hold, and charged past Cedwyn after Pellinore. Cedwyn covered the rabbit as the bratchet shot past. Guinevere made one last attempt to grab the hound but ended up face down in the dirt. Merlyn lay quietly—not sure why any of them still breathed—and tried to catch his breath. His hand rested on his chest, his breathing becoming easier as the pain lessened. Then he rolled over and inspected the children.

"Guinevere? Are you all right?"

"Ye..." She pushed herself up off the ground and sat down. Spitting the dirt out of her mouth, she looked over at Merlyn. "Yes, I'm all right."

"Cedwyn? Are you all right?"

Cedwyn had remained standing, a remarkable feat considering all that had just occurred. His head was buried in his arms. Dust covered him from head to toe. No sound came from him.

"Cedwyn?" Merlyn asked again.

Cedwyn glanced up and looked at each of them in turn. Guinevere's green tunic was covered with dirt and leaves. Branches were tangled throughout her hair. She looked like anything but a princess.

And Merlyn! Never had the magician looked so distraught! His hat askew. His normally neat beard full of leaves. His grey robe a filthy brown with a huge hoof print in the middle. Cedwyn, who looked as bad as they did, could hold it in no longer. He started laughing, careful not to open his arms. Soon Guinevere and Merlyn joined him, each pointing to the others' disheveled appearance.

Then with pride, Cedwyn slowly unfolded his arms. In his hands, the prize possession that he had protected throughout the melee: the rabbit!

That started the laughter all over again until none of the three could catch their breath.

"Well," Merlyn said, trying to regain his composure. "I guess we found Pellinore."

"Bet he doesn't get lost again, huh Merlyn?" Cedwyn said.

Merlyn merely glanced at him. He retrieved his pack from the ground and drew out a bag. Holding it open, he helped Cedwyn put the rabbit in and slung it over his shoulder.

"Follow me, please," Merlyn said, trying to sound like nothing out of the ordinary had just happened.

After brushing themselves off as best they could, Cedwyn and Guinevere followed Merlyn as he headed in the opposite direction from King Pellinore.

CHAPTER 9
LESSON OF THE RED DEER

The light darkened as the trees shut out the sun. Neither Guinevere nor Cedwyn had been this deep in the forest. They held hands as they fought to keep up with Merlyn. At each new sound, they moved closer together, afraid to be on their own.

"Guin'ver? Where do you think Merlyn is taking us?"

"I don't know. I thought we were just going to find King Pellinore." Up ahead Merlyn disappeared around a bend, dirt still clinging to the back of his grey robe. "Hurry. We can't let him get too far ahead."

Rounding the bend, they almost ran into him. He turned, and putting a finger up to his lips, motioned with his other hand to his ear.

Faintly, almost as if carried by the wind, came the soft sound of seemingly hundreds of tiny footfalls. Guinevere and Cedwyn looked at each other questioningly. Both shook their heads in unison. They had no idea who or what was making the noise or even what it was.

Merlyn's lined face softened with a smile. Silently he motioned them to follow him as he moved forward, carefully placing his feet soundlessly on the path.

They continued in this manner for several yards, the sound getting gradually louder. In the distance, the sunlight returned as the forest canopy became less dense. When Merlyn stopped, they could see a clearing up ahead, much larger than the one where they had tangled with the bratchet and the rabbit. Still smiling, Merlyn motioned them to follow him behind a large oak bush. Obediently they followed.

Crouching down, they looked through an opening into the clearing. A herd of red deer, so named because their hides took on a reddish tinge in the sun and moonlight, grazed quietly. The harts, or the male deer, fed on the outside of the herd, pausing frequently to check the wind for scents of danger. Merlyn again motioned to his ear. Listening, Guinevere and Cedwyn identified the sound they had heard earlier. The munching of the grass had sounded just like footsteps on the ground.

Merlyn motioned to his eyes and pointed to the herd. Looking closely, Guinevere and Cedwyn saw past the harts to the does and fawns inside, all eating quietly and contentedly. Although the red deer lived all around the castle, watching the herd eat as a family thrilled them. Several of the fawns, tired of eating and oblivious to danger, chased each other around and jumped in the air. Like good fathers, the harts let them play unless they wandered too close to the edge of the herd. Then, a quick nip on the neck or hindquarters sent the youngsters back into the center of the herd with a squeal.

"Merlyn," Cedwyn whispered. "How come the dads hurt the babies?"

Just as quietly, Merlyn answered. "They know that the only way to keep the does and fawns unharmed is to make sure that none venture beyond to where the harts cannot protect them. The gentle nipping is just a friendly reminder to stay within their protection, much like when you were younger and were not permitted outside the castle gate."

Cedwyn nodded and continued to watch, occasionally nudging Guinevere when a particularly rambunctious fawn tried to venture out too far. After half an hour, both children grew tired of watching. Crouching down behind the bush made their legs cramp, and none of the fawns broke loose or came any closer. Surprisingly, Merlyn shook his head when they motioned that they wished to move away. They looked at him closely. His blue eyes sparkling, he directed their eyes back to the clearing and the red deer. Deliberately, he mouthed the words, "Watch closely."

Curiously, they stared harder not sure what Merlyn wanted them to see. Guinevere saw it first—just a flash of white among the reddish brown. Her quick intake of breath signaled Merlyn and caused Cedwyn to tug on her sleeve,

"What?"

Guinevere motioned toward the deer. Cedwyn stared even harder. Then, so quick that he didn't think he had seen anything, he also spotted a streak of white.

A squeal erupted from the center of the herd. Suddenly, does and harts alike were scrambling about as a whirl of colors raced around the inside. While the three of them watched, the whirl of colors moved quickly toward the edge of the does and smashed through the barrier of harts!

Putting a finger to his lips, Merlyn cautioned them about crying out as the colors turned into individual animals. Out front and coming up only to the harts' underbelly, a fawn jumped and ran, trying to avoid the teeth of each hart it passed. Following the fawn came a white creature, no bigger than the fawn and just as playful. But where the fawn resembled the harts and does, the white creature did not.

Its tiny hoofed feet seemed to float across the ground. Each leap sent the mane of white and silver flying, and caused the forelock to get tangled around the horn in the center of its forehead. It took a minute or two for them to realize that they were looking at a baby unicorn. With their eyes as big around as a full moon and their mouths open, they watched as the harts herded the youngsters back into the safety of the herd.

Briefly, the does parted, revealing more unicorns, young and old, in the center. One of the unicorns came forward and gently nipped the baby on its hindquarters, reinforcing the discipline of the harts. The baby squealed and ran out of reach.

Merlyn motioned for them to follow him as he moved farther

back into the forest.

"Merlyn! Those are really unicorns!" Cedwyn gasped as soon as they stopped.

"Yes, they are," Merlyn chuckled.

"Guin'ver, did you see them?"

"Yes," she replied, glancing at Merlyn.

"Merlyn, how did you find them? Are there any more?" Cedwyn questioned nonstop. "Wait a minute! How come you aren't 'prised, Guin'ver?"

At Merlyn's nod, Guinevere replied, "I've seen a unicorn before."

"You have not!"

"No, really. The night of the feast for King Arthur I thought I saw something from a window. I went into the forest to see if I could find out what it was. Merlyn followed me and showed me a unicorn," she explained.

"And you didn't tell me!"

"I couldn't."

"What do you mean, you couldn't? We're friends! I'm gonna be your squire!"

"I forbade her from speaking about the unicorn because I did not want anyone to know," Merlyn told him. "The fewer people who know about them, the longer they will live in peace. They have an important place in this world and need to be left alone." He proceeded to explain to Cedwyn about the important antidote that unicorns provided. He also hinted that once the unicorns were gone, mankind would be battling diseases they might not be able to defeat on their own.

"Now," Merlyn said as he knelt down to look Cedwyn in the eyes. "You also must promise me that you will never mention the unicorns to anyone. You must not even hint that unicorns are real. When people stop laughing at you and start believing you, then they will start hunting the unicorns. That is something that must never happen. Unicorns are magical creatures, but once man hunts them, they will be destroyed. Promise me."

Cedwyn looked into Merlyn's eyes, assessing the sincerity of his words. Convinced that Merlyn spoke the truth, he looked up at

Guinevere. She nodded.

"I promise, Merlyn. I won't tell anyone or talk about the unicorns except with you and Guinevere."

"No. Once we leave here, you can't even talk to me or Guinevere about them, ever. You don't know who might be listening." He put his hands on Cedwyn's shoulders. "It has to be a secret that just the three of us know and that we hold in our hearts. Understand?"

"Yes."

"Good, any other questions?"

"Why are the unicorns hiding in the middle of the red deer?" Guinevere asked.

"Because the red deer promised long ago to protect the unicorns from humans and other creatures."

"But, why?" both asked.

"Well, it so happens that at one time the unicorns saved the life of the grandfather of all red deer."

"How'd they do that?" Cedwyn interrupted.

"Give me a minute, and I'll tell you," he replied, as he sat down on the grass. When they had joined him, he started his story.

"When the forest was young, many, many years ago, a red deer wandered here from across the water to the south. Not knowing the land, the red deer soon became lost, unable to find fresh water. The unicorns came across it dying of thirst. They nudged and pushed the deer to fresh water and later showed it the best grazing grounds and the safest places in the forest to bed down. Before long, the unicorns adopted the deer which, in turn, promised that all future generations of red deer would protect the unicorns.

"A few years later another red deer found its way here from across the same water and was discovered and saved by the first deer and the unicorns. The two red deer later mated and proceeded to start the herd that would protect the unicorns forever," Merlyn concluded.

"That's a long time to keep a promise," Cedwyn said.

"Not really when you look at this land we live in. For hundreds of years the common people of this land have pledged their allegiance to a king. The king protects them, and the common people

93

fight for him. There is little difference between what the red deer promised the unicorns and what people throughout time have promised their king."

"So, when the people promise to fight for King Arthur, that's the same thing?" Guinevere asked, slowly understanding Merlyn's message.

"Yes, it is. And even Cedwyn here has done the same thing."

"Me?"

"Guinevere has promised to take you with her as her squire. In turn, you pledge to be loyal to her and fight for her. She then vows to care for you and protect you."

"Really, Guinevere?" Cedwyn asked, looking at her with new respect.

"I suppose so," she replied, realizing some of what would be expected of her.

"So when Guinevere marries King Arthur, he will protect her?" Guinevere looked to Merlyn.

"He will do his best. But people are a bit different from animals. Your parents already try to protect you, but what happens sometimes?"

"We don't do what they say and get into trouble," Guinevere mumbled.

"And even hurt," Merlyn finished. "People are like the baby unicorn back there. Even though you try to protect them, often the choices that they make put themselves in danger."

Both remained silent while they thought about what Merlyn had said. Their eyes strayed to the herd and each thought of what might have happened had the baby unicorn made it to the trees and someone other than themselves had been watching.

"How can people be sure to make the right choices?" Guinevere asked.

"With people, it's always a struggle. The best thing that you can do is to follow your heart. It seldom leads you wrong." Merlyn's sad smile revealed his inner turmoil. Your heart was not supposed to be wrong, he knew, but sometimes it just happened. Unfortunately, he knew both he and Guinevere would find that out one day.

CHAPTER 10
EVE OF LEGEND

O ne year later.

The two of them moved slowly through their familiar hunting ground. Cedwyn, taller than a year ago, lowered the bow and wiped the sweat off his forehead. Guinevere stood watching silently.

Raising the bow and nocking the arrow, he started to pull back his arm and stopped.

"What?"

No answer.

"Cedwyn," she said. "Will you shoot the arrow?"

"I'm trying to keep my arm steady like you said."

"The longer you hold the arrow nocked, the more unsteady your arm gets," Guinevere explained again, losing her patience.

He dropped the bow down and released the tension on the arrow. Then, transferring the arrow to his left hand, he clenched and un-clenched his fingers, releasing the pressure and stiffness in them.

"I'm never gonna be strong enough to hold the bow steady," he said.

"Sure you are," she reassured him. "Come on. We'll practice for a while longer and then see if we can find us a rabbit."

Cedwyn grinned. Positioning the bow and arrow, he shot and missed. His target, an old rotten ash off to the left, was in no danger.

For the rest of the morning, Guinevere dutifully retrieved the arrows. One time, Cedwyn's arrow went wild and the birds in a scrub oak several feet away scattered. Both laughed at the quickness of the birds.

"Remember last year when you accidentally shot the boar?"

"Yes I do," she replied with a smile. "I remember someone screaming that his foot was stuck, and he couldn't get loose!"

"And I remember someone up in a tree screaming each time the boar butted the tree!"

"We were lucky that day."

"And many other days also," he replied laughing. Then he reached for his bow and arrows. "Just a few more shots. I'm getting hungry."

Guinevere nodded and continued helping him work on holding and aiming the arrow until he finally got it right.

"Look! I hit the tree!"

She reached over and patted him on the back, marveling at how much he had grown in a year. Now when they stood next to each other, he almost reached up to her shoulders. That was no small feat, for she herself had grown almost two inches, standing just over five feet.

"See, I told you that you would be able to do it."

"But not without your help. What am I going to do after next year when you get married to King Arthur and leave the castle?" he asked, sitting down on the ground.

She knelt down beside him. Without thinking, she tousled his blond hair, now shoulder length.

"You'll be almost ten when I marry King Arthur. I told you before that you'll come with me and be my squire."

"But I won't be old enough. And besides, you could choose any of the older boys."

"Yes, I could. But you are my friend. We can't stop having adventures just because I get married. I mean, I shall have some duties, but I suspect I will also be alone while King Arthur is out protecting the country. I will need a friend. And besides, my father has asked your mum to come with me when I move to Arthur's castle."

"Really?" At her nod, he threw his arms around her shoulders with joy and then stood up. "Are you okay with becoming a queen?"

"Most of the time," she said getting to her feet. "I still get a little scared when an important visitor shows up, and I have to talk to them. But my Latin," she grimaced, "is getting better since I started practicing more. And learning how to run a castle has been more interesting than I thought." She glanced up at the cloudless blue sky. "I told your mum that we'd be back early. Let's go and see if we can find a rabbit for Cook."

"Guin'ver,"

"Yes?"

"I'll try to be real quiet."

"I know you will."

"Guin'ver?"

"Yes?"

"When is King Arthur coming back? Will he be here for your Birth Day?"

"Not this year," she replied, smiling at the thought of seeing him again. Like her father promised, through Arthur's visits over the past year, the two had become friends. Guinevere found herself saddened that Arthur would miss her Birth Day, but she knew that his numerous journeys to the north country were very important. "He's up north and promised to stop by on his way home to Camelot in a month or so."

"Is Merlyn comin' this year with more fireworks?"

"I don't think so. When he left last year, he said that he would be busy helping Nimue, the lady who takes the unicorns." Guinevere clamped her hand over her mouth.

"But we aren't supposed..."

"I know. It just slipped out," she answered, relieved no one else was around.

"I sure will miss the fireworks."

"Me too, but he promised that for my fifteenth Birth Day he would bring a huge surprise."

"I can hardly wait."

"Yes, but that's a year away, and right now I'm getting hungry. Let's see if we can find a rabbit to bribe Cook into giving us a late breakfast." Picking up their bow and arrows, they walked closer to the forest.

The two presented quite a sight. Cedwyn, still very much a young boy even at eight, bounced alongside Guinevere. He stopped frequently to shade his eyes from the sun as he peered up ahead, looking for signs of a rabbit.

Guinevere had not only grown taller over the year, she had matured. The women of the castle even considered her beautiful like her mother. Her long brown hair had lost its childish fuzz. Still braided, its fullness and softness framed her tanned face. She didn't quite bounce and skip as she had done a year ago, but her steps maintained their spring and determination. She looked and acted very much like a queen.

"Look over there. Where the sun just touches the forest."

Guinevere stopped and looked closely.

"See where the grass is swaying?" Cedwyn dropped his voice almost to a whisper.

She nodded and reached for the arrow he handed her.

"Hold your arm steady," he whispered.

She glanced at him, a frown starting to wrinkle her smooth creamy skin.

He grinned at her, and her frown disappeared, replaced by a grin. She sighted her arrow, keeping an eye on the feathers, and let it fly. They watched the arrow sail straight and then dip down and drop into the long grass.

A murderous squeal filled the clearing. They looked at each other and then back to where the arrow had disappeared. Tall grasses bent violently with the swift movement of an animal. In a moment, they knew what had happened and did not hesitate.

Grabbing the bow and arrows, they shouted as one.

"Run!"

EPILOGUE

On her fifteenth Birth Day, Guinevere became engaged to King Arthur. During the year that followed, the two, already good friends as her father had predicted, fell in love. They married shortly after her sixteenth Birth Day. Unfortunately, Guinevere was too young to understand the feelings she felt for Arthur and confused friendship with love.

Several years later, as a woman of twenty-five, true love came to her in the form of Lancelot, a French knight who had become Arthur's best friend. Their love, the world believes, destroyed King Arthur and Camelot. In truth, their love was just one of many things that contributed to that downfall.

And what about Merlyn? He, like Guinevere, found out that frequently the heart makes its own choices. Merlyn fell in love with Nimue, that kind lady who helped the unicorns. In the end, he discovered she only wanted his powers. Once she had those, she imprisoned Merlyn in a cave for the rest of his life.

AFTERWORD

Before the written word, tales of a brilliant warrior leader and his followers who excelled above all others were passed down: tales of King Arthur, Sir Lancelot, and The Knights of the Round Table and their quest for the Holy Grail.

The most famous written accounts of King Arthur start in the twelfth century with Geoffrey of Monmouth's Historia Regum Britanniae (History of the Kings of Britain). Sir Thomas Malory's Le Morte d'Arthur (The Death of Arthur), written in the fifteenth century, provides readers with some of the most colorful and detailed narratives of the Knights of the Round Table and jousting ever recorded. In the modern age, one of the most popular versions of the Arthurian legend was written by T. H. White. His The Once and Future King found its own slot in history with the making of the animated The Sword in the Stone by Walt Disney in the 1960s. This rebirth in modern cinema continued with Excalibur, First Knight, and King Arthur in 2005.

It is not easy to explain the continued popularity of King Arthur and his Knights of the Round Table. Some believe that the honor and justice exhibited by Arthur and his Knights are what is needed to right the wrongs of the world. Some believe so strongly in the quest for the Holy Grail that they have patterned their lives after these knights. Some just enjoy the days of old when knights defended the land and rescued damsels in distress. Still others from as far back as 1190 have spent their entire lives just trying to prove that King Arthur did or did not exist.

Whatever the reason, the legend of King Arthur keeps recurring throughout the ages in written format, in the world of entertainment, and has spread throughout the Internet. Its appeal, like the character, is ageless.

GLOSSARY

Amphora-a two handled wine vessel; usually large but also copied in smaller versions for drinking glasses

Anvil-a heavy iron block used by blacksmiths to shape iron

Bailey-the inner courtyard of a castle surrounded by a defensive wall

Blacksmith-a person who uses water and iron to make weapons, pots and pans, and shoes for horses

Bratchet-a hunting hound (dog)

Cornish hens-a breed of tamed birds raised for meat; also found in the wild

Caldron-a large cooking pot, usually blackened from its use over a fire

Circlette-small cakes with almonds and currants baked inside and covered on the outside with fresh raspberry jam

Doe-a female deer

Hart-a male deer

Keep-the central tower of a castle, usually the strongest

Lyre-a stringed instrument similar to a harp but smaller

Moat-a defensive ditch surrounding the outside of a castle and/or town filled with water to prevent enemies from entering

Nock-putting the bowstring into the grooved end of an arrow in anticipation of shooting the arrow

Painted Dragon-a strange looking creature with skin of many colors; one of the creatures hunted by King Pellinore

Parapet-a low wall inside and below the main wall surrounding a castle; used by archers to defend the castle; easily accessible for people inside the castle

Parchment-writing paper prepared from an animal's skin

Red Deer-a deer with a reddish-brown coat

Round Table-made famous in Arthurian literature as the table in which King Arthur's knights sat around and no one was sitting higher or lower than another and where there was no seat more important than another; also called a table of equality

Tunic-a woman's gown-like garment with or without sleeves that can be long enough to touch the ankles or short enough to be worn over a skirt or pants

KING ARTHUR
LEGEND

Sometime between 600 and 800 A.D., King Arthur was born out of wedlock to King Uther Pendragon and Queen Igraine. Upon his birth, Merlyn the magician took Arthur away to be raised by Sir Ector, a knight and landholder. Growing up on Ector's estate, Arthur did not know that he was of royal birth. Merlyn watched Arthur's growth closely because he knew that one day Arthur would be a great king.

Upon the death of King Uther Pendragon, there was no one to take over the throne. Merlyn did not want to reveal Arthur's heritage because the boy was still too young. He buried King Pendragon's sword Excalibur up to its hilt in a stone and then declared that whoever pulled the sword out of the stone would be the rightful king of the Isle of Briton. Hundreds of men tried to pull out the sword, but could not. And so there was no king, and for many years, there was no protection for the English people from renegade kings trying to gain control over more land and people.

Once Merlyn decided it was time, Arthur was sent to the stone where many of the kingdom's people stood waiting. He walked up, grabbed the sword's hilt, and with little effort pulled Excalibur from the stone. From that point on, King Arthur ruled over the Isle of Briton. To bring order back to the country, he founded the Knights of the Round Table, which included the famed Sir Lancelot. It was the Knights' duty to enforce the laws and to punish the wrongdoers.

Arthur married Guinevere when she was just a teenager, himself not much older than 20. Together they ruled from Camelot, and Briton prospered. It was only when long-forgotten prophecies came to pass that Arthur's kingdom faltered and eventually failed. But the people did not forget the world that Arthur had brought them. Forever in history he is known as the once and future king: the king who will come again when the world is ready.

As for Merlyn, he was a very different magician. He lived backward in time. In other words, he lived in the future first and then he lived in the past. What this meant was that Merlyn knew the events that were going to happen because he had already lived through them. While this would appear to be good knowledge to have, he was unable to change the events in the past to avoid the future. This was particularly unsettling for him because he knew that he would be imprisoned by Nimue, but he could not stop that from happening. He also saw, but could not stop, the fall and rise of Arthur, and the betrayal Sir Lancelot and Guinevere.

Questions for Discussion and Enrichment

1. Guinevere was betrothed or promised to Arthur on her thirteenth Birth Day in an arranged marriage. Mary, in Chapter 3, can hardly wait to be betrothed. Research what countries in the world today allow arranged marriages. At what ages are the girls betrothed?

2. Describe the differences in the lives of Maggie and Guinevere. How is your life different from one of your friends?

3. Go back to Chapter 2 and review what Guinevere learns in her schooling. How does your education differ from hers? How is your education similar to hers?

4. Unicorns are common in fantasy literature. Find another legend about the unicorn.

5. In Chapter 9, Merlyn explains about the relationship between red deer and the unicorns. He likens it to the relationship between a queen or king and their people. Where is this type of arrangement between rulers and their people found today?

6. Legends, like King Arthur, are stories that have lasted century after century. Using the internet, find two other legends and give a brief explanation of them.

ADDITIONAL READING

Le Morte d'Arthur. Malory, Sir Thomas. Originally published 1485.

Tales of King Arthur Illustrated. Malory, Sir Thomas. Edited 1981.

The Once And Future King. White, T.H. 1965.

What Life Was Like In The Age of Chivalry, Medieval Europe AD 800-1500. Time-Life Books, 1997.